WITHDRAWN

THE EXTINGUISHED GUEST

A LEXIE STARR MYSTERY NOVEL

THE EXTINGUISHED GUEST

JEANNE GLIDEWELL

FIVE STAR
A part of Gale, Cengage Learning

GALE
CENGAGE Learning

Detroit • New York • San Francisco • New Haven, Conn • Waterville, Maine • London

GALE
CENGAGE Learning·

LIBRARY OF CONGRESS CATALOGING-IN-PUBLICATION DATA

Glidewell, Jeanne.
    The extinguished guest : a Lexie Starr mystery novel / Jeanne Glidewell.
        p. cm.
    ISBN-13: 978-1-59414-896-5
    ISBN-10: 1-59414-896-1
    1. Middle-aged women—Fiction. 2. Bed and breakfast accommodations—Fiction. 3. History—Societies, etc.—Fiction. 4. Wild bird trade—Fiction. 5. Missouri—Fiction. I. Title.
    PS3607.L57E98 2010
    813'.6—dc22   2010025163

First Edition. First Printing: October 2010.
Published in 2010 in conjunction with Tekno Books and Ed Gorman.

Printed in the United States of America
1 2 3 4 5 6 7 14 12 11 10

Dedicated to my Grandma Dolly, aka Mary Van Sittert, who passed away recently at 94 years young.
I miss her greatly.

ACKNOWLEDGMENTS

I'd like to thank my agent, Mike Valentino, of M&R Literary Associates in Cambridge, Massachusetts, my friend and editor, Alice Duncan, of Roswell, New Mexico, and my friend and writing mentor, Evelyn Horan, of Temecula, California. I'd also like to express my gratitude to Five Star Publishing and thank my friends and family for their support and encouragement, and especially my husband, Bob Glidewell, and sister, Sarah Goodman.

CHAPTER ONE

I turned over for at least the hundredth time in my quest to find a comfortable sleeping position, but the mattress had less give than a concrete runway at Chicago's O'Hare Airport. I'd have to convince Stone Van Patten, my boyfriend and proprietor of this recently renovated inn, to buy featherbed mattress pads for the beds. Harriet's Camelot B&B in Schenectady, New York, where Stone and I'd become acquainted, had down-filled mattresses and to me, sleeping on a down-filled mattress was like sleeping on a cloud. I'd seen this kind of mattress pad selling on the Internet for less than a hundred dollars, and if Stone wanted repeat customers, his investing in comfortable bedding would be money well spent.

I'd be lucky if I didn't end up covered in bruises from all the flopping around and flipping from side-to-side in my attempt to fall asleep. I just knew I'd be groggy and out-of-sorts while trying to perform my duties as Master of Ceremonies at the induction dinner, honoring Horatio Prescott III, the new president of the Rockdale Historical Society. The induction ceremony was being held in conjunction with Alexandria Inn's grand opening. Stone had been thrilled when approached with the idea by the club's secretary, Patty Poffenbarger.

Having no luck in falling asleep, I considered taking one of the four sleeping pills I'd been carrying around and hoarding for nearly twenty years. But like every other time I'd thought about taking one, I talked myself out of it. Instead I opted to save them for a more critical occasion—when getting a good night's sleep was of life-altering importance—even though my pills were on the verge of disintegrating into dust.

"What am I saving them for?" I asked myself, feeling disgusted with my neurotic tendencies. I hated to admit it, but I'd fried pork chops with more sense than I sometimes exhibited. Could I be saving the pills for the restless night before I gave my presidential inauguration speech, or perhaps on the eve of my wedding day when I was to marry a foreign prince? Was it so I could be well rested and alert before blasting off in a space shuttle to orbit some far-off planet in a distant galaxy? For goodness sakes, I was Lexie Starr, a widowed forty-eight-year-old, Midwestern library assistant. I led a normal, sedate life in the suburbs of Kansas City, and mine was a life not exactly riddled with important, life-altering occasions. I wasn't apt to be accepting an Oscar, an Emmy, a Pulitzer Prize, or even the neighborhood award for "Lawn-of-the-Month."

I sighed and turned over once again, knowing that should I meet with a situation worthy of one of the antiquated sleeping pills, they'd be less than useless, anyway, and totally ineffective from being several decades past their expiration date, if not merely little piles of powder. I might just as well have flushed them down the toilet immediately following their acquisition many years ago. That was shortly after the unexpected death of my husband, Chester, when I was not yet thirty years old. He died suddenly of an embolism when our only child, Wendy, was seven years old. It'd been her and me against the world for the next twenty years, but we'd persevered and survived.

I was thinking about the transition I'd made back then, to being a single mom following my husband's death, and I was finally drifting off to sleep when a loud noise broke through the night's silence. The resounding thud came from the ceiling directly above my bed. I sat straight up in alarm. It sounded as if someone had dropped a sixteen-pound bowling ball on the floor above me, or perhaps had fallen out of bed while flopping around, as I'd been doing most of the night. I was quite sure whatever caused the sudden loud noise could not be a normal occurrence.

I glanced over at the alarm clock on my nightstand. There were less than two hours before I had to be up and about if I were to be dressed and ready to help Crystal prepare breakfast for our guests by seven-thirty. Falling asleep now might be worse than not sleeping at all.

I considered going upstairs to investigate the loud noise, but like with the sleeping pill, I talked myself out of it. It was never a smart idea to go waltzing into a stranger's room at 5:08 in the morning. That would be a good way to find yourself waking up dead—from being shot as an intruder with questionable intentions.

I rolled over, forcing the curious thoughts about the predawn thud from my mind, and soon fell into a light slumber.

My fear of being shot as an intruder must have been prophetic because as it turned out someone did wake up dead that morning, even if that someone wasn't me. And the "deadness" was indeed the direct result of a gunshot wound. The victim was our distinguished guest of honor, Horatio Prescott III. But Mr. Prescott couldn't have been accidentally shot as an intruder because he was found murdered in his own room. After he'd failed to show up for breakfast, Stone and I went upstairs and found him, face down on the floor, next to the window overlooking the flower gardens outside. I assumed he'd been killed at approximately 5:08 A.M. and was surprised to see he was already dressed for the day in a dark gray, pinstriped, three-piece suit. As it drained from a single bullet hole in the back of his head, a pool of blood had formed beside his body. It was a gruesome sight, forever imprinted in my memory.

While I studied the scene, I saw a ballpoint pen in the victim's right hand. There was a look of amazement frozen on his face as rigor mortis set in. I surmised the killer had utilized a silencer on his weapon. I'd heard a distinctive thud-like sound that would have been made by Prescott's stout, compact body hitting the floor. But I was positive there'd not been an audible bang preceding the thud, like the sound of a bullet being fired into the back of the man's bald head. I couldn't recall any other sounds, such as two men wrestling over possession of a weapon. I had a hunch that Horatio Prescott had been taken completely by surprise and was dead the second after he realized he was about to be killed.

Looking down at the rigid, prostrate body, I felt a moment of guilt and regret. Perhaps if I'd gone upstairs to investigate the noise as I'd considered doing soon after I'd heard the thud, Mr. Prescott could have been saved with the assistance of emergency medical technicians. Perhaps, even, the killer who'd offed Mr. Prescott could have been apprehended, or at least identified, had only a mere minute or so been allowed to pass following the fatal shot. But then, perhaps the killer who'd offed Mr. Prescott could have panicked and also offed the middle-aged library assistant who, out of idle curiosity, was schlepping up the stairs in an oversized K.C. Chiefs' football jersey she called a nightshirt. Seems it may have been a damned good thing I was able to persuade myself to ignore the noise and stay under the covers in my rock-hard bed for another two hours!

I looked around at the roomful of people standing with their mouths agape, stunned expressions showing on their faces. They were the other Historical Society members, and all were obviously as shocked as I. This was certainly not included on the copy of the schedule of events I'd been given the night before.

From across the room, Stone caught my eye and shrugged in

disbelief. After checking Mr. Prescott's neck for a pulse for the sixth or seventh time, Stone lifted the phone from the night-stand and punched in nine-one-one on the handset. He motioned for me to herd all of the guests out of the room that had now become a crime scene. He may have been afraid the Historical Society was about to become the hysterical society, once the severity of the matter sunk in.

Stone instructed everyone to refrain from touching or disturbing anything in the room. I wasn't sure if Stone was trying to protect any evidence that might be present from contamination or protect the reputation of the Alexandria Inn he'd recently purchased. It was an antebellum mansion located just north of St. Joseph, Missouri. Stone had restored and named the historic inn after me. The inn had just opened for business the previous day, and a murder was not a particularly auspicious beginning for the lodging establishment. It was memorable, maybe—but probably not conducive to enticing hordes of customers to register at the inn, taking their chances on being shot dead in the middle of the night. The exalted guest-of-honor, Horatio Prescott, had been assigned the most luxurious suite the inn of-fered. Unfortunately, I feared, the impressive suite would forever after be known as "site of the murder" and not deemed very desirable.

"Come on, Cornelius," I said softly, as I nudged Mr. Walker toward the door. Nearby, I tapped the bony shoulder of the regal and sophisticated-looking Rosalinda Swift.

"Let's go make some coffee, Ms. Swift, while we wait for the police and coroner to arrive. We're obligated to preserve the purity of the crime scene, I'm sure. There's nothing we can do now for Mr. Prescott, anyway."

I nodded at the Poffenbargers as I watched Patty Poffen-barger absentmindedly bite the end off a chocolate long john dangling from her right hand. I was amazed she could even think of eating at a time like this, although she probably ate out of habit most of the time, without much thought about the food she was ingesting.

"Humph!" Patty said indignantly after she had licked the icing from her fingers. She glared at Stone with a look of accusation. "If I'd known something like this was going to happen, I would've made arrangements for the Society to stay elsewhere. What kind of establishment is this?"

I wanted to defend the Alexandria Inn because I realized Horatio Prescott could have been killed at any lodging facility in town. Actually, what I really wanted to do was slap a piece of duct tape across Patty's mouth. Instead, I counted silently to ten, took her by the elbow and led her across the room, with her husband trailing behind us. By my estimation, Patty would tip the scale at three hundred pounds, while her six-foot tall husband, Otto, couldn't have weighed over a hundred and twenty pounds, even wearing a heavy winter parka with its pockets full of rocks. It's not that I have anything against people who are heavier than they really ought to be—I was a bit on the pudgy side myself—I just didn't like anyone making negative remarks about the Alexandria Inn, a business we had worked hard to make successful.

Harry and Alma Turner were standing in the corner of the oversized room. Gesturing, I caught Harry Turner's attention. Trembling slightly, Harry leaned against the wall, as Alma stood next to him and dabbed at her eyes with a pink, flowery handkerchief. I waved the dumbstruck Turners out the door behind Rosalinda Swift, Cornelius Walker and the Poffenbargers, and as a group, we marched woodenly down the hallway to the staircase.

We passed Robert and Ernestine Fischer on our descent downstairs. I explained the situation and quickly turned the elderly couple around to go back to the parlor with the rest of us. The only guest unaccounted for was the overbearing and pompous man I'd met yesterday, Boris Dack, whose room was across the hall from mine on the first floor. Mr. Dack must have overslept, I concluded, as we passed his closed door on the way to the parlor. Like Mr. Prescott, Boris Dack hadn't appeared for breakfast at the appointed time of seven-thirty. His "Do Not Disturb" placard still dangled from the doorknob of his room. No one claimed to have seen him yet that morning.

As the ever-gracious host, I was helping Crystal dole out croissants and pour fresh cups of coffee a few minutes later. I wondered who'd want to kill Horatio Prescott III on the very day of his induction as president of the Rockdale Historical Society. Was the killer someone who coveted the honorable position and was determined to have another crack at it? I found it hard to fathom why anyone would actually want the position. I couldn't imagine nominating anyone for the position except out of spite or pure orneriness. I'd rather sit through a root canal than be thrust in that position.

Did the killer have an entirely unrelated grievance against the dead man? Could it have been a stranger who'd clandestinely entered the Alexandria Inn in the wee hours of the morning, shot the prestigious Mr. Prescott, and then exited the building unobserved?

Or was the killer, instead, one of the nine other guests registered at the Alexandria Inn? All the guests were acquainted with Horatio Prescott III and, in fact, had been specifically invited to be a part of the induction ceremony. All but Alma Turner, who was attending the event with her husband, were members of the Historical Society. Could one of them have a reason to despise the man enough to kill him? Could one of them have convincingly faked surprise at finding Mr. Prescott dead in his room? Would the killer be identified and brought to justice? I knew I couldn't rest easy until these questions had been answered.

My first impression of Horatio Prescott had been that he was a refined, fastidious but unassuming gentleman. But I really knew very little about him or any of the other nine guests making up the small, local Historical Society. However, I had a sneaking suspicion, somehow, in some way, this was all about to change.

CHAPTER TWO

"Ms. Starr, are you certain you read the clock and remember the time correctly? You'd have been barely awake, alarmed, and possibly disoriented," Detective Wyatt Johnston said as I poured a refill into his coffee cup. In my severely anxious state-of-mind, I sloshed coffee over the edge of the cup onto the kitchen counter. The detective absentmindedly wiped the spill with the sleeve of his blue shirt and gazed at me with unwavering eyes.

"I was completely awake at the time, Detective Johnston, I assure you. I have occasional bouts of insomnia, and last night it was kicking in at full force."

"Any particular reason for your insomnia? Were there unusual noises keeping you awake?"

"Like an argument or a life-and-death scuffle in the room above me?" I asked.

"Uh-huh, something of that nature." Detective Johnston shrugged and nodded with an expectant expression, as if convinced I'd heard such things and was suffering temporary amnesia. I knew he was going to be disappointed if I didn't have something more sensational to add to my statement.

"No. Sorry Detective, but I heard nothing of the kind."

"Okay," he said, obviously not convinced. "We'll come back to that later."

"I think she couldn't sleep because she needed a man beside her," came from a squeaky male voice behind me. "She was no doubt frustrated and unsatisfied."

I was flabbergasted by the remark as I looked up into the rheumy eyes of Cornelius Walker. I wasn't sure I'd heard him correctly. Was he unaware that the proprietor of this inn was my boyfriend? Then he winked at me through his thick, horn-rimmed glasses, with one of his bloodshot, watering eyes, and I nearly dropped the carafe of coffee on the floor. I started to make a sarcastic reply, but he spoke again.

"I think Dr. Walker has just the prescription she needs to make her sleep like a baby, Detective," the innocuous-looking, sixty-something-year-old man said, totally oblivious to my revulsion.

I glanced over at the policeman's amused expression and then back at Mr. Walker, who winked at me again and crossed toward the parlor. He was a short man, just a couple of inches taller than I, maybe five-four or five-five at the most. He wore plaid polyester slacks and had thinning, greased-back hair, large, prominent ears, and a slender build. I thought he looked more like a library assistant than I did.

As Cornelius walked out the kitchen door, Stone walked in, nodding politely at the slightly older gentleman as they passed.

"Stone, did you hear what he just said to me?" I asked, in complete astonishment.

"Who?" Stone asked with a chuckle. "Horny Corny?"

"Horny Corny?"

"I've heard several guests call Cornelius that, but not to his face, of course. Late yesterday evening, I heard him ask Rosalinda Swift if she'd like to 'participate in some passionate parlor games' with him. He suggested 'tonsil hockey' or 'spank the monkey' and for a moment I actually thought she was going to pass out 'with the vapors.' " With the last few words, Stone had raised his voice in perfect imitation of Rosalinda's. I laughed at his mockery.

"Horny Corny's a very fitting moniker, but he looks so, so . . .

well, so harmless."

"Oh, I'd imagine Cornelius is harmless enough. He's just desperate to draw attention to himself. A man like Mr. Walker tends to blend in with the wallpaper if he doesn't make a substantial effort to be noticed. I'd bet if some woman was to go along with one of his off-the-wall sexual comments and respond in a positive manner, he'd be the one on the verge of fainting," Stone said.

"You might be right, but just in case you aren't, I don't think I'll test your theory. Is the guy really a doctor?"

"No," Stone said, as he laughed louder this time. "He's a fertilizer salesman or something. That's why he's so full of it."

Detective Johnston, who'd been silently drinking his coffee and listening to the exchange between Stone and me, started laughing, too. I'd almost forgotten the policeman was in the room. He leaned back in his chair and said, "Actually, he's a floor manager at the Farm and Ranch Supply store in downtown Rockdale, but he does sell fertilizer in his department. I had to pick him up once on some kind of charge for 'lewd and lascivious' behavior. We found out later that the woman he'd been groping was actually a man—a transvestite in drag. Talk about rubbing salt in a guy's wound. The charges eventually got dropped, but all of us guys down at the station got a good laugh out of it."

"I'm sure you did," I said, somewhat annoyed at the detective's attitude. "Sorry, I never did answer your question, and by now I've forgotten what you were asking me about earlier."

"I believe I was asking you about the exact time you heard the loud thud and if there was a reason why you were awake at the time. Most people are sound asleep at five in the morning." Detective Johnston was like a pit bull gnawing on a bone.

"Didn't hear a thing, other than the victim hitting the floor, huh?"

"That's right. That's all I heard. There's no particular reason I was awake, other than the mattress on my bed is harder than my last batch of cookies."

Officer Johnston nodded as he fiddled with the squelch control on his police radio. Stone looked at me with an apologetic expression and said, "Sorry, Lexie. I've been meaning to buy some new mattress sets for all the beds, but I've had so many other irons in the fire, I just haven't gotten around to it. The one on my bed's pretty uncomfortable, too."

"No sense buying entire mattress sets, Stone. All you really need are featherbed mattress pads to place on top of the existing mattresses. I noticed some nice ones on the Internet for about ninety bucks apiece. The mattresses are even baffled."

"Baffled?" he asked, with a comical expression of confusion on his face.

"Quilted in such a way to keep the feathers from bunching."

"No kidding?" Stone considered the idea for a moment. "Can you order some for me if I give you my credit card number?"

"Sure. I'd be more than happy to order some for you."

"Thanks for the suggestion. It would save me a bundle. A king-sized mattress and box springs can run over five hundred, easily."

"Easily," I said, in agreement, before turning back toward the other man in the room. Somehow we had gotten distracted from the pressing matter of Prescott's murder. "By the way, Detective Johnston, has Mr. Prescott's next of kin been notified?"

"I'm not sure. I know he's not currently married, and his parents are both deceased, but he does have a daughter named Veronica, from his first marriage. Still lives out in Utah, last I heard. She was in my graduating class. She was drop-dead gorgeous, but she always acted like she thought she was better than the rest of us and never had much social interaction with anyone in the class. She always looked at me as if I was something her cat hacked up. I'd heard she married a guy from a Mormon family in Leavenworth, but I never met him."

"And she moved to Utah with her husband?" I asked.

"Yeah, just outside Salt Lake City," Wyatt said. "Hey, I noticed Rosalinda Swift's name on your guest list. I had to arrest her recently, too; it was on a DUI a couple of weeks ago. She was three sheets to the wind and just missed running over a small child on a bike. It was only about four in the afternoon when I pulled her over."

"Rosalinda Swift? Are you sure it was the same Rosalinda Swift from the Historical Society?" I couldn't quite picture her behind the wheel of a car, three sheets to the wind, as the detective put it. "She was drinking and driving?"

"Uh-huh. She was weaving all over the road, from one shoulder to the other."

We chatted with the police officer about Rosalinda and Horatio's daughter Veronica and also the unfortunate and mysterious demise of her father for about ten more minutes before the officer had to leave to respond to a domestic abuse call. Before he left, he asked Stone if he'd inform all of the guests that it would be appreciated, but not necessary, if they could all stay at the inn for a few days while the investigating team took statements and collected evidence. He'd already taped off Mr. Prescott's room as a crime scene and had assigned a couple of detectives who were busily dusting for fingerprints and searching for clues and potential DNA evidence. One slim young recruit was fingerprinting everyone who was on the premises when the murder occurred. I noticed Rosalinda Swift was quite agitated by this indignity. She finally agreed to the "humiliating procedure," but not without significant complaining. Only Patty Poffenbarger appeared more offended than Rosalinda by the request.

Stone was completely cooperative with the detective squad and readily agreed to speak with his guests about staying over a day or two—at no expense to them, of course. As Wyatt Johnston backed his squad car down the driveway, Stone answered his ringing phone. He listened to the caller for a moment and shook his head in bewilderment. After a few brief comments, he re-cradled the phone with more force than normal.

"News travels fast in a burg like this, doesn't it?" Stone gave a sigh of disgust and ran his fingers through his silver hair. "Now I know what they mean by a small town's 'grapevine.' That was a reporter with the *Rockdale Gazette,* wanting details on the murder and my opinion concerning who might have committed it. Does he really think I would open myself up to slander and libel charges by naming names? I told him I couldn't make any comments at this point, but I can see it now on the front page of the paper tomorrow, the headline 'Local inn opens with a bang.' "

I knew Stone was discouraged and dejected. It was a matter of personal pride to him to see the Alexandria Inn be success-ful. He'd paid a handsome price for the rundown old mansion and had pumped a lot of money into restoring it.

I'd met Stone while I was on the east coast last fall, investigat-ing the unsolved murder of my son-in-law's first wife, Eliza Pitt, a case in which my son-in-law, Clay, was a prime suspect. I'd had no investigative background or training, but I felt it was necessary to do whatever I could to protect my daughter, Wendy, from possibly suffering the same fate.

Stone, an online jeweler whom I'd contacted to help me replace a charm bracelet and charms that Wendy had recently lost, offered to assist me in my investigation. The two of us had formed an instant bond and found we had much in common.

We'd both been widowed for years—he's fifty-five, and I'll turn forty-nine soon—and we'd met at a time when we were both finally ready to consider having another "significant other" in our lives.

We decided to pursue the relationship, and after his father, suffering with Alzheimer's, died in December, Stone sold his jewelry business to an employee and moved to the Midwest to be near me. Before heading west, he'd also resigned his volunteer position as a reserve police officer for the Myrtle Beach Police Department, a service he'd chosen to help fill his idle time.

Lacking serious hobbies, Stone wasn't the kind of man who could sit around and do nothing. He became interested in operating a bed and breakfast after staying at the Camelot B&B in Schenectady and helping the owner, Harriet Sparks, make some repairs around the place. In Missouri, he discovered the old deteriorating mansion in nearby Rockdale by accident, while scanning the classifieds in the *K.C. Star* newspaper. He quickly made the decision to purchase it and restore it to its original, elegant condition. The project was a massive undertaking, but Stone appeared to enjoy the challenge immensely.

Once the job was completed, he succeeded in having the mansion listed on the National Register of Historic Places. Then he hired a young woman named Crystal to serve as combination cook and housekeeper and opened it as a fully functional and operating inn. He christened it after my given name, Alexandria Marie, which pleased me immensely. The Alexandria Inn, located in the small town of Rockdale in northwestern Missouri, was about an hour's drive from my home in Shawnee, Kansas. It was ideally situated in the heart of the heavily populated historic district, with homes built during the late 1800s, but the inn was only a half dozen blocks from the business district.

Stone enlisted my help in decorating and furnishing the inn while he supervised the crews doing most of the actual restoration. Between us, we managed to give the home its original dignity, charm, and beauty. Stone stayed busy at the inn during the week, but we spent the majority of the weekends with one another. So far the arrangement had worked out perfectly.

Stone was not a classically handsome man. He was of average height and carried a few extra pounds on his waist, but it was his personality more than his looks I found so attractive. He was attentive, witty, and considerate. His smile lit up his face, despite the small gap between his two front teeth. His silver hair and almost translucent blue eyes added an air of refinement. He was a "glass half full" type of guy, and his optimism was contagious. Being with him tended to give me a more tolerant attitude, too. And tolerance wasn't a trait I came by naturally.

Wendy, my twenty-seven year-old daughter, had moved back home with me following the annulment of her marriage to Clay Pitt. Living with me was a temporary arrangement, she said, while she saved money on a down payment for a place of her own. She worked with the local coroner, primarily assisting with autopsies. To me, the job seemed a bit gruesome and depressing, but she appeared to enjoy it. She'd managed to put a few extra pounds on her too-thin body and was looking more relaxed and contented than she had in many months.

I took special pains to prepare all of Wendy's favorite dishes since she returned home and was sleeping in her old childhood room once again. In the process of eating such meals, I put on seven or eight pounds myself and was now about fifteen pounds heavier than I should be for my height, despite my good intentions to lose weight. I carried the weight well and wasn't fat, by any means, but I was on the verge of becoming plump. And "plump" and "chubby" were not adjectives I liked to have tacked on to my physical description.

Stone didn't seem to be concerned about my increasing weight—would probably not even notice until I got to be the size of Patty Poffenbarger, which I vowed was never going to happen. Never mind gastric bypass, I'd personally sew my lips together with monofilament fishing line before I'd allow myself to swell to that extent. To me, being grossly overweight was as self-destructive as smoking, and I'd been able to wean myself off cigarettes after years of the lethal habit. I didn't want diabetes, heart disease, or hypertension any more than I wanted lung cancer or emphysema. There was no reason I couldn't lose the extra pounds and get back down to my normal, desired weight if I set my mind to it. Wendy, on the other hand, had to fight to keep weight on her slim frame.

I was relieved Wendy had formed an instant affinity with Stone. She talked frequently on the phone with his nephew Andy, whom we'd both met in New York. Andy was a pilot who owned a five-passenger Cessna and flew private charters. He lived near Stone's former home in Myrtle Beach, but he'd recently mentioned a desire to move to the Midwest to get away from the hustle and bustle of the east coast. He yearned to live out in the country and told Wendy he wouldn't be totally contented until he had to kick manure off his cowboy boots before entering his ranch house.

I knew Wendy was attracted to Andy. She was doing all she could to encourage him to make the move to the Midwest. He was a good-looking young man, as thoughtful and admirable as his uncle, and I hoped, in time, something more permanent would develop between the two of them. I would be proud to have Andy as my son-in-law.

I looked over at Andy's uncle, Stone Van Patten, who was now deep in thought.

"Stone?"

"Yeah?" he said.

"I have an idea."

"Uh-oh. Go ahead, I'm listening."

"Why don't the two of us do a little investigating ourselves?"

His light blue eyes gazed into my light brown ones for several seconds before he smiled. "Well, it's an intriguing idea," he said. "We do make a pretty good team, don't you think?"

"Detectives Smith and Wesson," I said with a nod, teasing him about the fictitious names he'd given us during a subterfuge encounter we'd had with a bar owner in Boston during our previous investigation into the murder of Eliza Pitt. "It couldn't hurt anything, I guess. We don't have anything to lose, do we?"

"No, not really."

"And if we can help figure out who killed Horatio—and why—it could only be advantageous to the success of the inn."

"I agree, honey," Stone said, after a few moments. He reached out absentmindedly and tousled my short, brown curly hair. It was a reminder I needed to make an appointment for a fresh perm some time in the next week or two. I had worn my hair in the exact same style since I was a senior in high school, and there was no reason to switch to a more "en vogue" style now. Stone put his hand back on his lap and continued talking.

"I don't want people to be afraid to stay here. The fact that Prescott's death occurred here is just a coincidence. But it'll be difficult to convince people not to associate the inn with the murder."

"Well, then, I say let's go for it. If nothing else, it should make for an interesting experience."

CHAPTER THREE

Staying on at the Alexandria Inn for a few more days seemed to be no problem for the Historical Society guests, aside from Boris Dack, who had urgent business matters to attend to but could still spend the majority of his time at the inn. It was Monday, and most of the guests had planned to stay for several days and depart on Wednesday or Thursday. Even though the induction of a new president had been postponed for obvious reasons, they had nothing else on their schedules.

Most of the guests lived within minutes of the inn but were treating the occasion as a mini-vacation, an opportunity to let others cook for them, wait on them, and, in general, treat them like visiting royalty. Although they certainly had vastly different personalities and temperaments, they all seemed to have one thing in common—they enjoyed "putting on the dog" and being made to feel like first-class dignitaries. They liked the feel and the illusion of importance. They wallowed in it, in fact.

Crystal, Stone, and I went out of our way to assure our guests continued feeling as if they were celebrities because they found it a satisfying arrangement. Satisfied customers were repeat customers—and word-of-mouth was the best, most cost-effective kind of advertising. After all, it was hard to beat free when it came to being cost-effective.

We learned quickly, however, to succeed in the accommodations' industry, we had to be accommodating. Being polite was expected, and necessary, no matter how much it irked us to be treated as subordinate minions by people with no higher perch on the caste totem pole than our own.

Thank goodness for Crystal, a professional hostess, who didn't appear to resent being ordered about by a bunch of hoity-toity old snobs. She scurried among the guests with a tray full of refreshments in one hand, a coffee carafe in the other, and the pockets of her apron filled with sugar packets, napkins, spoons, and toothpicks. She provided everything guests could need before they even realized they needed it. She kept everyone's coffee cup filled, and encouraged the ingestion of far too many doughnuts and pastries. Patty Poffenbarger seemed quite fond of the young woman, or at least, she was seldom very far from her. When Patty wasn't running off at the mouth about her own accomplishments as a concert pianist, which were probably greatly embellished, she was filling that mouth with refreshments from Crystal's ever-present tray of goodies.

At least Patty's husband, Otto Poffenbarger, didn't appear to have an inflated opinion of himself. He was, in fact, almost abnormally self-deprecating, similar to a child who is told daily how stupid or worthless he is. He stuck to his wife Patty like a postage stamp, as if he were afraid if he lost sight of her he'd immediately dissolve into nothingness. He followed her around like a shadow, so closely I feared if Patty ever made a sudden, unexpected stop, Otto would become a human wedgie. I thought if I looked up the word "hen-pecked" in the dictionary, there might be a picture of this poor, pitiful man.

Boris was on the other end of the spectrum. He was the most irritating, overbearing individual I'd ever had the displeasure to meet. Stone discovered from Boris Dack, that Boris was Horatio Prescott's business partner, the "D" in "D and P Enterprises," a business involving investments, both foreign and domestic.

Boris's body reminded me of a bowling pin; bottom heavy with sloping shoulders and wide hips. He had thick, bushy white hair on the sides of his head, but only about seven strands of hair on top. The hairs on top were several inches long and had a tendency to stand straight up like a flag mast. His large, bulbous nose reminded me of Jimmy Durante's, and his eyes were a piercing charcoal color.

Boris also had an ego the size of Mount Rushmore, and if you didn't agree with something he said, he would repeat it over and over, and louder and louder, until you finally gave up and agreed with him. He spoke with great authority about anything and everything, occasionally using words that even Noah Webster wouldn't recognize. I'm certain Boris thought they made him sound more intelligent, more respectable. I thought they made him seem childish—like a young girl trying on her mother's makeup and clothes.

Boris was the only guest who found it necessary to leave the inn, but just for a few hours, he promised. He had several business-related obligations to take care of early Tuesday morning, he'd told Stone, but he would return later in the day. With the death of his business partner, there'd understandably be many details he'd need to handle in the near future. Stone assured Boris he'd be allowed to come and go as needed.

"Pardon my soliloquy, but I am appalled by the iniquitous deportment evinced by a member of the Society. It's execrable!" Boris said.

Later I asked Stone to decipher the statement. He thought a moment and said, "Boris was thinking murdering Prescott was a shitty thing for someone to do."

"Now that's putting it in layman's terms," I said.

"The question is, why did Boris indicate it was one of the guests who killed Horatio? Does he know something, or is he just making natural assumptions?"

"I wondered about his implication, too. And his attitude seems odd to me."

Boris Dack's behavior seemed too unfeeling for a man professing to be devastated by the loss of his friend and associate. I placed him high on my list of suspects and was eager to delve deeper into his business "relationship" with Mr. Prescott.

"Lexie, can you come into the kitchen for a minute?" Stone asked. "I've got something I want to discuss with you for a few minutes. Crystal can take care of the guests while you take a much-deserved break. You'll wear yourself ragged, if you aren't careful."

I was pouring Earl Grey into a dainty little teacup, like a well-trained servant, and as I turned toward Stone's voice, I was haughtily dismissed by a wave of Rosalinda's blue-veined hand. She and Mrs. Poffenbarger were enjoying brunch in the parlor, away from the distasteful discussions about the dreadful murder that had occurred right under their upturned noses that morning. Ms. Swift was sipping her fourth cup of the fragrant tea. I noticed she'd added something to it from a small, sterling silver flask she'd extracted from her sequined purse. Patty Poffenbarger, dressed in something resembling a purple, polka-dotted pup tent, was preoccupied with stuffing the last of a half-dozen poppy-seed muffins in her mouth.

"What's up?" I asked Stone when I entered the kitchen.

He handed me a cup of espresso, which he knew I preferred over tea or weak coffee. "Have a seat," he said. "You're still serving 'your highnesses,' I see."

"Yes," I said. "And what a couple of snooty old windbags they are. If I hear about that damned encore at Rosalinda's last recital one more time, I'm going to—"

"I know, I know. I'm sorry, honey. I really didn't intend for you to have to serve and wait on these people. Crystal's doing her best—"

"—I know. Crystal's terrific, but she can't be in six places at the same time. And I don't mind, Stone. Really I don't. I find their high-faluting behavior kind of amusing, in a way. And besides, I owe you a favor for all you've done for me."

"Lexie, you don't owe me anything. I can hire another—"

"No, that's not necessary, and I didn't mean it quite the way it sounded, Stone. But let's just say I'm enjoying myself and I want to help and leave it at that. Now what did you want to discuss with me?"

"Well, okay, if you're sure. It was never my intention to have you serving as Crystal's assistant. Anyway, I spoke with the investigating team upstairs and found out a few interesting details that I thought you'd want to hear."

"Like what?"

"First of all, the only fingerprints they could find in the room besides the victim's were the expected ones—yours, mine and Crystal's. So that's of no help. But they did make an observation that might prove useful."

"What was that?"

"As you may have noticed, we got about two inches of snow last night. The snow fell between midnight and three A.M." There was a certain quality of smugness in Stone's voice I'd never heard before. I knew he was enjoying the resurgence of our sleuthing partnership. He enjoyed a challenge as much as I did.

"And?" I prompted.

"There were no footprints in the snow between the house and the street. Just a few incidental prints between here and the house next door, leading up to the front porch from the side yard rather than the sidewalk. The investigators took a few photos of the prints, but don't feel too strongly they have anything to do with the murder. They think the footprints may have been from the shoes of an officer who reported to the scene when I called nine-one-one for assistance."

"So, what's the significance?"

"No sign of intruders. Don't you see? It looks very likely that Mr. Prescott was killed by someone staying in the inn. Otherwise, there'd most likely be footprints leading out to the street."

"Oh."

"And also there are no signs of a forced entry. I remember checking all the doors last night after the guests retired to their rooms and once again, just before I went to my own room. That makes it even more probable that the killer is among our own little covey of quail," Stone said. He watched me as his words soaked in and then asked, "Got any thoughts or ideas?"

Did he mean other than the fact I'd be rearranging the furniture in my room tonight so that it was all piled strategically in front of the door? I'd also most likely be placing a fingernail file under my pillow because it's the closest thing I possessed to a lethal weapon. Gee, and I had thought insomnia was a problem last night?

"Well, Stone, I know I didn't like Mr. Dack's attitude or his demeanor this morning when he found out his business partner had been killed. He expressed feelings of sorrow and grief, but he didn't show a lot of physical anguish at the news. And he didn't appear to be overly stunned, either. He seemed a little too matter-of-fact about the whole thing to me. And why did he oversleep? Could he have been up doing dastardly deeds in the middle of the night?"

"It's possible, I guess. But how could a guy kill someone in cold blood and then slip back into bed for a few extra zees?"

"I don't know, but I think we need to have a talk with him. Feel him out if we can."

"I agree, but we're not official investigators, Lexie. He's under no obligation to tell us anything, you know. We'll have to approach this in a clever fashion."

"Oh, I think we can find clever ways to get the answers we're looking for."

"Hmm. Why does your tone of voice alarm me?" Stone asked.

"No guts, no glory."

"Glory's for young guys who are in better shape than I am," Stone said. He lifted up the carafe to warm up my coffee, and as he poured it, he asked, "Say, did you know Rosalinda Swift was once engaged to Horatio?"

"You've got to be kidding!"

"No, it's true. Or, at least it's true according to Robert Fischer, who's known Horatio for years. He said the two were engaged for several months about fifteen years ago, but Horatio broke it off when Rosalinda refused to sign a prenuptial agreement. Since the engagement debacle, the two have pretty much just ignored each other—in public, anyway. But Robert thinks there's a chance Rosalinda's carried a grudge against Horatio all these years for degrading her by even asking her to sign the agreement, and then embarrassing her even more by calling off the engagement. Perhaps she decided to exact a little revenge—retribution for the public humiliation she suffered."

"He humiliated her and embarrassed her to the point that fifteen years later she put a slug in his brain? No, I don't really think so, Stone. A crime of passion that takes place fifteen years after the fact? I just don't buy it. No scorned woman would wait that long to exact justice."

"Okay. I think it's a little far-fetched, too, but it wouldn't hurt to check into Rosalinda if we get a chance. We don't want to make any assumptions that could prove to be wrong."

"You're right. We probably should try to do an inquiry into what kind of relationship each of the guests had with Mr. Prescott. We don't want to overlook some seemingly insignificant detail that later turns out to be a key factor in his death."

I went to my room for my Minolta Maxxum camera. I wanted to get my own photos of the footprints outside, just in case they became significant later on in the investigation. Unfortunately, when I went outside to take the pictures, I discovered the sun had melted most of the early morning snow. Only two footprints still remained, one from a left shoe and one from a right. They were in the shade of a shrub on the north side of the front porch, where the snow was only beginning to melt in the late morning's warmth. A warm front was pushing through, I'd heard on the radio, and more seasonal temperatures were forecast for the early-spring day. The front would be short-lived, however, with another winter storm on the horizon.

I photographed the footprints from several angles, noticing the right print looked misshapen, narrower than the left print just inches away. The right portion of the footprint must have been melting faster, I concluded, perhaps from having less weight applied to that side when the print was made. From the placement of the two footprints, it appeared the individual making them had walked to the side of the inn's front porch from the neighbor's yard or the carport, while staying on the red concrete landscaping stones bordering several raised flower gardens, until just before reaching the porch. The landscaping stones were almost dry and completely free of snow. Between the neighbor's yard and the flowerbeds was the Alexandria Inn's carport, where two of the squad cars had parked earlier. As the investigating team had surmised, it seemed probable the prints belonged to a responding officer who had pulled up to the carport upon arrival. If so, the officer had smaller than average feet, for the footprints were not made by large feet. It shouldn't be difficult to determine if any of the responding officers had small feet. The suburban town of Rockdale had only four or five police officers on its payroll.

I jotted a quick note on a pad of paper I'd crammed in the pocket of my sweatshirt jacket. I wanted to remember to ask Stone if, by chance, he'd noticed any tire marks in the driveway or carport prior to the arrival of the officers. It didn't seem logical to me that someone with the intention of breaking into the inn to kill a guest would blatantly steer his car up the drive and park it in the carport while executing the murder. It was more logical to park on the next block and sneak up to the house from the alley behind the building. I decided to check the back of the house. Because most of the backyard was still in the shadow of the house, the snow there had barely begun to melt, and there were no signs of footprints leading to or from the alley or anywhere near the back porch or sidewalk.

I snapped a couple of photos of the undisturbed layer of snow blanketing the backyard before noticing Robert Fischer sitting in a padded, wrought-iron chair on the back porch. He wiggled a couple of fingers at me, and I wiggled a few back. He was wearing a bright orange jumpsuit like you'd expect to see on a member of a chain gang picking up trash along a busy interstate. He'd worn a brown suit when I'd first seen him that morning, but he had changed into something more comfortable. A well-worn pipe dangled from his lips. Mr. Fischer looked very calm and collected, as if murder were an every day event in his life.

Thinking this would be a perfect opportunity to pump him for information, I walked over and sat in the other porch chair identical to his.

"How are you doing? I'm Lexie. You're Mr. Fischer, aren't you?"

"Yes. Robert Fischer. And I'm doing fine, young lady. How are you?"

"I'm okay. Are you staying outside to try to escape the hubbub inside?"

"Yes. I didn't figure I had much to tell the investigators that would be of any help. I didn't see anything, didn't hear anything," he said. He laughed in a mocking manner, and added, " 'Course I take my hearing aids out when I go to bed at night, and without them I couldn't hear an elephant fart in a metal bucket."

I smiled and then noticed there was no smoke coming from Mr. Fischer's pipe as he inhaled repeatedly on its stem.

"Your fire's gone out, Mr. Fischer," I said, pointing at the barrel of his pipe.

"Robert, please, or Bert if you'd like. What's your name again, little lady? My memory is not as good as it used to be."

"Alexandria Starr, but please call me Lexie."

"Lexie, ahhh, I see. Hence, the 'Alexandria' Inn."

"Yes." I smiled at the congenial old man.

"Well, Lexie, I gave up smoking about a dozen years ago. Or, I should say, I gave up tobacco, but not the pipe. Got tired of Ernestine yapping at me about the health hazards of smoking, and I decided to avenge myself by outliving her and marrying some fluffy, big-breasted twenty-year-old after the old nag's dead and gone."

I wasn't sure how to respond to that remark, so I didn't. Instead, I smiled inanely and nodded my head. Eventually, sensing my discomfort, the octogenarian chuckled and told me he'd only been joking with me. Suddenly an expression of chagrin flashed across his face as he realized his inappropriate choice of words. He waved his hand back and forth, as if trying to erase the callous remark about his wife, and said, "Please forgive me for being so insensitive. I meant that as a joke. I wasn't thinking—"

"That's okay. But Ernestine's right you know," I interrupted, excusing his untimely quip in an attempt to ease his embarrassment. "Smoking is a slow form of suicide, and I'm glad you were able to quit. I kicked the nasty habit a few years ago myself. I walked around with a lollipop in my mouth for weeks, until the inside of my cheek was almost permanently puckered, so I imagine still having the pipe in your mouth, even without actually smoking tobacco in it, makes it easier for you to—"

"Nah, not really," he cut in. "I just happen to think the pipe makes me look more sophisticated."

I laughed, but Robert didn't, so I wasn't sure if he was joking again or not, but I decided to get down to the business at hand.

"Stone said you told him that Mr. Prescott and Ms. Swift were engaged to marry years ago. Is that true?"

"Uh-huh."

"Seems like such an unlikely match to me."

"Well, no, not really. Our Ms. Swift was a remarkably attractive woman in her prime, and Horatio appreciated anyone in a skirt who had more curves than brains. Rosalinda had her own reasons to find the partnership attractive, one being that she was heavily mortgaged at the time. She'd borrowed a lot from the bank to make costly home renovations and was actively looking for a solution to her money problems. And as a former banker, I know that to be the truth. I handled both of their accounts the last year or two before I retired. Somehow Horatio discovered she was a gold-digger, and he closed the mine, so to speak."

"How did they meet? Do you know?" I asked.

"They were both divorced, and both owned homes in the historic Museum Hill District of St. Joseph, houses dating back to the late eighteen hundreds. Rosalinda's home is a Victorian like this one, designed by the locally famous European architect, E.J. Eckel, and Horatio's was an Italianate mansion. Still a part of his vast holdings, last I knew. I'm fairly certain the two met through the Historical Society. Like Horatio, there are a number of people who live in St. Joseph but belong to the Rockdale

Historical Society, preferring the less formal, more intimate atmosphere of a smaller club."

"Is that how you originally met them, as well? Through the Historical Society?"

"Rosalinda, yes, but Horatio, no. I'd known him for years. Like I said, until I retired in 1985, I was a loan officer at the Rockdale Bank and Trust, and Horatio's been doing business with that bank forever, I think. Even before I took over his and Rosalinda's accounts, Horatio was on the board of trustees at the bank."

"Were you friends?"

"Acquaintances," he said, in a manner indicating distaste. "But never friends."

"You didn't care for him?" I asked, maintaining a casual, conversational tone.

"No, not particularly. And I certainly didn't trust him or have a lick of respect for him."

"Why's that?" I was careful to be interested, but not notably so. I knew I had a tendency to nail people to the backs of their chairs with my single-minded intensity if I didn't hold myself back.

"Long story, but about twenty years ago I was endeavoring to purchase a large parcel of land in downtown St. Joseph. Perhaps you've noticed that vacant lot right on Main Street? I thought it'd be a good investment for my retirement. I'd made an offer and was waiting to see if the buyer was going to accept it or make a counter-offer. Horatio just happened to come into the bank that day and asked me to go to lunch. We'd had lunch together on several other occasions, so this was not an unusual invitation. During the meal, I casually mentioned my intentions, as well as the amount I'd offered the buyer, and the reasons I thought the property would greatly appreciate in value in the following few years. It would cost me nearly every dime I could scrape together, but I thought it would be worth the sacrifice later on.

"To my surprise, I received a call later that day. I was told the buyer had taken the property off the market. Naturally, I was disappointed, but I accepted it as something that just wasn't meant to happen. I didn't give it a lot of thought at the time. I eventually invested the money in some stocks that performed well over the years and netted me a tidy profit."

Robert grew silent, pausing to take a few smokeless puffs on his pipe.

"Go on," I urged when he didn't continue speaking.

"Well, come to find out, Horatio bought the property the very afternoon that we'd lunched together. Offered the buyer a few hundred bucks more than I had for the property, and the buyer accepted his offer. Of course, a hundred bucks went a lot further in those days. But the buyer hadn't actually taken it off the market. He'd just sold it to the highest bidder, who just happened to know exactly how much it'd take to outbid me."

"Wow, that was a low blow, wasn't it?"

"Rather unprofessional and underhanded, yes. But par for the course for Prescott, from what other folks have since told me. I was only one of many people who have been swindled or outwitted by him over the years. Even his business partner, Boris, claims Prescott tried to bilk him out of many thousands of dollars, his share made on some foreign commodities that D&P Enterprises had invested in and sold for a hefty profit. And it's not like I'm under any illusion that Boris Dack is a saint, either."

"Wow, it's no wonder someone wanted to kill Mr. Prescott."

Robert looked at me then with a curious expression, and said, "It didn't upset me to a degree of that magnitude, I promise you. I didn't dislike him enough to go to prison for killing him. In fact, I think the whole thing ruffled Ernestine's feathers more than mine, and she's no murderer either. It especially irked her when the property was recently selected as the site for the new shopping center, and Horatio was promised six and a half million clams for it. They are surveying the property right now, doing title search work, and ironing out the details of the contract."

"Goodness sakes! That's a lot of money, isn't it?" I said. "Phew! Surely your stock investments didn't perform quite as spectacularly, did they?"

"No, but they're adequate enough for our needs. And yes, it will be an incredible return on Horatio's money, I assure you. His heirs will be delighted, no doubt."

"So Ernestine wasn't too fond of Prescott?" I asked, in a thinly veiled attempt at prying. I wasn't overly concerned with anyone's constitutional rights. It was easier for me to consider every guest guilty until proven innocent.

"Ernestine considered Horatio to be crude and uncouth. He'd made a habit of referring to us as 'Bert and Ernie' in public, which infuriated Ernestine even further. She felt it was very disrespectful. He's gone now, and I look at the whole matter as water under the proverbial bridge, but it taught me not to trust a man like Horatio any farther than I could throw a water buffalo."

I smiled at the vision his remark invoked. And I had to agree with Ernestine's assessment of Horatio Prescott. The Sesame Street reference was childish, and being snookered out of six and half million bucks might ruffle anybody's feathers, I thought.

I patted Robert's forearm, shook my head in disapproval, and said, "Well, Robert, I can see why Ernestine felt the way she did about Mr. Prescott. It doesn't sound like Prescott was a man with much integrity or very high morals."

"No. Sadly, he wasn't very principled for a self-proclaimed

God-fearing man. He was an elder at the Presbyterian church, as well."

"Jekyll and Hyde syndrome?"

"I think he felt as if his duty at the church would erase his misdeeds in the eyes of the Lord, and perhaps ease his conscience at the same time," Robert said.

"Hmm . . ."

"I'm sure there was a motive behind it. Horatio makes . . . er, made, very few moves that weren't calculated. Which explains, in part, anyway, the wealth he amassed over the years."

"As wealthy as he apparently was, he must have kept a substantial amount of money in the Rockdale Bank and Trust."

"A substantial amount by most people's standards, but the bulk of his amassed fortune is in Swiss accounts. A lot of his wealth comes from questionable sources, like black market trading. There have even been rumors of a mob connection. So my guess would be a lot of the money has been nicely cleaned and pressed—"

"Huh?"

"Laundered," he clarified.

"Oh, my. And Boris? Is he aware of this?"

"Oh, I'm quite certain he is. In fact, I'd imagine he's the man with the soap!"

CHAPTER FOUR

Robert dumped imaginary ashes beside his chair and then placed the well-worn pipe in a back pocket before excusing himself to re-enter the Alexandria Inn. I noticed while we talked that he'd been shivering from the cool March wind as it flapped the thin, orange material of his jumpsuit back and forth against his skin. He was a tall, lanky gentleman, with a slightly bent-over posture, and was probably in his mid to late eighties. He was much too thin. There wasn't much meat on his bones to insulate him against the cold.

I was feeling a bit chilled myself and lifted my camera from the table to go inside when I heard the distinct squeak of the patio door opening again. Patty Poffenbarger, holding a pastry, liberally covered in powdered sugar, swept out onto the back porch with her very reticent spouse in tow. They each carried a cup of steaming coffee Crystal had probably just refilled.

I was beginning to think of Otto and Patty as Jack Sprat and his wife. If Otto could eat fat, he wasn't eating enough of it. He made Robert Fischer look beefy in comparison. And if Patty, who easily outweighed Otto by a hundred and seventy pounds, could eat lean, she was apparently not too fond of it, or she was eating enough of it for six people.

"Otto, sit there!" she instructed, as she pointed at a barren, brick flower planter. Otto obediently sat down on the edge of the planter and immediately dug his hand into the potting soil, which I had recently prepared for the planting of spring flowers.

He let the soil sift through his fingers, studying its quality. "Needs potassium to be more fertile," he muttered. "A little potash and nitrogen, too."

Patty, meanwhile, had plopped her large frame in the chair Robert Fischer had recently vacated. I held my breath as the chair groaned but, fortunately, didn't collapse. She was wedged in tightly, filling every inch of it, and I wondered if it might require Crisco and a crowbar to extract her from it.

"Doing okay?" I asked.

"Fine, fine," Otto said, without even a glance in my direction.

Patty looked astounded, as if she couldn't quite believe her husband had the audacity to respond in such a manner or had even taken it upon himself to respond at all. She leaned forward and said, "We're not fine, Otto, not fine at all. We're being held here and made to look like criminals in the eyes of all Rockdale's citizens. I'm sure at this very moment we're being gossiped about all over town. I know all the members of my bridge club must think I'm a suspect in Prescott's murder, and I don't know how I'll ever face any of them again. It's humiliating to the core, Ms. Starr. Rosalinda Swift agrees totally with me about this, I might add. It is a travesty of justice, and I, for one, intend to sue somebody for this assassination of my character."

With a dramatic "Humph!" and a lot of exertion, Patty pushed herself back into the chair, which made creepy sounds as if struggling to support her weight.

"Oh, my, Mrs. Poffenbarger, I'm so sorry you and Ms. Swift feel that way," I said. Why did I feel I had to coddle this whiner when I really just wanted to slap the self-righteous look off her face? "I'm sure the detectives will let you leave if you prefer not to stay at the inn. Detective Johnston said it was a request, not a demand, and intended only to simplify matters."

"Humph!" Patty Poffenbarger repeated.

Slap, slap, slap, I said to myself.

"You and Mr. Poffenbarger are not suspects, nor is Ms. Swift, and I don't think anyone is under the impression that you are. The detectives just need to question you in case you heard or saw anything that might be useful in their investigation. That's really all there is to it."

"If we were to leave, we'd look like we were hesitant to speak with the investigators. As if we had something to hide," Patty said. "Isn't that right, Otto?"

Otto looked up, cocked his head and shrugged. "Yes, dear."

It was obvious to both him and me that Patty didn't really care about his opinion. He immediately went back to running his fingers through the soil in the planter.

But Patty had made a point I couldn't dispute. I know I'd move them up the ladder on my own suspect list if they refused to cooperate with the investigating team. "It will probably only be for one more day, anyway," I said. "They've already taken statements from Stone and me and a few of the guests, and fingerprints from all of us. Remember, Stone and I are in the same boat as you. I was the first one to be questioned, in fact. Besides, Mrs. Poffenbarger, would it be all that horrible to have to stay here one or two more days? It's what you had originally intended to do anyway, and now the accommodations are complimentary, and you'll be able to enjoy a little unexpected rest and relaxation."

"Oh, I suppose that's true," Patty said in resignation. She picked a coaster up from the sofa table and began to fan herself. "Goodness, it's hot!"

"Would you like me to get you some ice water or something?" I needed to go inside and get some more coffee, anyway. If it did nothing else, it would warm me up a bit.

"No, it's likely just a hot flash. This stress we're under is not good for me. I have a thyroid problem, you know. It's under-active, you understand—Hashimoto's Thyroiditis, the condition is called. It's the reason I have to contend with a few extra pounds. And I think it's been acting up this morning because I feel a bit light-headed, all of a sudden."

A few extra pounds? A hundred and fifty extra pounds, she must have meant to say. At least it was a comfort to know the sugar-covered pastries I'd helped Crystal deep-fry earlier had nothing to do with those "few extra pounds" Patty had to contend with.

"Yes, quite faint, actually. Perhaps I do need a little something to boost my metabolism." Patty's voice had dropped to a near inaudible level, as if the very effort of speaking normally was too much for her and her under-active thyroid. "Could you run to the kitchen and see what you can find for me to nibble on?"

"Yes, Mrs. Poffenbarger," I said.

"Yes, dear."

Otto and I had answered in unison. I motioned for Otto to sit down, and then waved to Crystal, standing beside the window and peering out at the porch. She instantly appeared at Patty's side and offered the tray of refreshments, as if by habit. She rolled her eyes as Patty selected several cream-filled doughnuts from the tray, while lamenting about her thyroid condition. I had to stifle a giggle as I watched Crystal refill the Poffenbargers' coffee cups. There was enough caffeine being consumed at the inn to the degree no one in the entire household should be able to sleep for a week. I poured myself another cup of the fragrant beverage before Crystal left to check on the rest of the guests.

To make idle chatter, I pointed toward a raised flowerbed in the backyard where small, light purple blossoms were poking up above the fresh layer of snow. "Look at those colorful little flowers out there. Poor things bloomed a little too early, didn't they?"

"Actually, they're right on schedule," Otto said. "Those are called snow crocuses, my dear. They always bloom in early spring and often come right up through the snow, hence, their name. With their violet petals, grayish veins, and yellow throats, I'd say those are what are known as 'firefly' crocuses."

I guess the surprise showed on my face. Patty explained matter-of-factly, between licks of the Bavarian crème oozing out onto her fingers, "Otto's a botanist. He usually spends most of his day in a lab, staring at silly old plants."

It was obvious Patty thought this was the most ridiculous waste of time imaginable, but as an amateur gardener, I was interested in "silly old" plants, too. "Do all of the crocuses come up this early in the spring?" I asked Otto.

"Well, the snow crocus, of course, comes up in early spring, as do most of the crocuses. But there's also an autumn crocus, found primarily in Europe and the Middle East. It blooms in autumn and bears fruit in the spring. All parts of that particular plant, however, are lethally poisonous."

"Really?" I was genuinely intrigued by Otto's knowledge.

"Yes. It has useful aspects though. The bulb of the autumn crocus contains the alkaloid colchicin, which is still used to treat gout. It's also used in genetics because of its property to cause polyploidia."

"Polyploidia?"

Patty was yawning, but apparently content to let her husband discuss insignificant matters with the feeble-minded maid while she polished off the doughnuts. I had to stifle my own sudden desire to yawn.

"Having a chromosome number that is a multiple greater than two of the monoploid number—"

"Oh, I see." I had no clue what he was talking about, but I cut him off because I didn't really have the time or desire to listen to the entire scientific spiel on polyploidia. It was clear I'd misjudged Otto, who didn't look as if he had two brain cells to keep each other company. Jack Sprat or not, Otto Poffenbarger was obviously a highly intelligent individual.

"I'm impressed, Mr. Poffenbarger," I said, as Patty shook her head in obvious disgust at my laudatory remark. "You should think about writing a book."

"Well, actually, my dear, I *am* writing a book—but it has nothing to do with botany. It concerns my other interest—restoring historic homes. How to do it properly so as not to destroy the innate historical quality of the structure. There's nothing more distressing than finding an old Tudor mansion decorated with Victorian furniture from a later period, or any historic home being restored with features from a different era than when the home was actually built. Did you know the flying buttress evolved during the Gothic Era?"

"No, I didn't, but I do see your point. It sounds like such an interesting subject. I'm sure your book will do extremely well once it hits the book stores."

"I doubt it, but it stands to do better, now that Mr. Prescott is deceased."

"Huh?" I asked, taken back by his unexpected remark. "What do you mean by 'now that Mr. Prescott is deceased,' Otto?"

"He was working on a book about the same subject, but he'd progressed much farther than I in its completion. It looked like his book would hit the market well in advance of mine, thereby diminishing the success of my book. A first-rate publisher had just offered him a contract, in fact. I haven't even queried agents yet."

"Did he begin his book first?" I didn't mean to imply that Otto had stolen Horatio's idea or was being a copycat, but he seemed offended by my question. Even Patty appeared irritated, but this was more likely spurred by her annoyance at my display of interest in her husband's book, a subject she obviously found boring beyond belief.

47

"He certainly did not!" Otto said, with more emotion than I'd have thought he possessed. "I started my book weeks before Prescott even thought of the idea. In fact, I truly think he got the idea from me. Unfortunately, Horatio required much less sleep than I do. Maybe three or four hours to be completely refreshed, but I require a full eight hours of rest each evening. He told me once that he awoke at about four most mornings and worked on his book until breakfast and then off and on, whenever he could throughout the day. My job doesn't allow me such luxury. I can only devote a few hours each evening to my writing. His book's progress soon overtook mine."

"I see," I said. The main thing I suddenly "saw" was the reason Mr. Prescott was already up and dressed for the day at 5:08. He must have been up working on his manuscript about restoring old homes when the killer entering his room interrupted him. There was a ballpoint pen in his hand at the time of his death. I didn't recall a manuscript being discovered at the crime scene, however. I would have to inquire about this, whenever the opportunity arose.

"Shut up, Otto, you're boring me plum to death," Patty said. She pointed a half-eaten glazed doughnut at me. "And her too, I'm sure."

"Yes, dear," Otto replied, and resumed his sifting through the potting soil in the planter.

CHAPTER FIVE

I stood up, made a couple of comments to the Poffenbargers about the weather, frostbite, and having work to do in the kitchen, and walked back into the inn. Passing the door to the parlor, I heard Crystal speaking to Boris Dack. I was shocked to hear venom in her voice as she said, "If you weren't so self-absorbed, Mr. Dack, you'd see I was busy pouring coffee refills."

"What'd you say?" he asked, obviously surprised by her uncharacteristic attitude. "You cheeky, little—"

"You heard me! If you need an ashtray, go to the kitchen and get one for yourself. I spend half my time trying to keep them cleaned out, as it is. Some people don't appreciate the smell of nasty, old cigar ashes, you know."

I was as taken aback as Boris. I would've never expected Crystal to stand up to the domineering man the way she had. She was usually very patient and able to brush off anything and everything demanding guests said to her. She probably was in desperate need of a little respite, I concluded. The young woman had been rushing around all morning in her attempts to take care of everyone's needs. With a pleasant lilt in my voice I spoke through the parlor door. "Crystal, my dear, it's time for you to take a much-deserved break as soon as you get a chance."

"Yes, ma'am," she replied. "I'm ready for one."

"I'm sure you are. You've been working hard all morning."

I continued down the hall. As I passed the library, I looked through the glass doors and noticed Harry and Alma Turner sitting side by side in the ornate mahogany loveseat that Stone and I had discovered in an antique shop in the nearby town of Weston. They were both absorbed in the books resting on their laps, and were so identically positioned, they looked like human bookends. I hadn't had a chance to speak with the pair since they'd registered, so I decided to spend a few minutes with them now while I had the opportunity.

I was reaching for the doorknob when I sensed, rather than felt, a hand brush across my backside. I wasn't positive it had even happened or had been intentional if it had, so I didn't know whether or not to be affronted when I saw Cornelius Walker slide by me on his way to his own room. I chose to ignore the gesture on the chance the tenuous groping had just been a figment. I was tired and stressed out, and my imagination might have been working overtime.

"Let me know if you need help sleeping tonight," he said with a wink as he opened the door and quickly disappeared. He was gone from sight before I could respond, which was just as well because I'd been rendered speechless by his remark, which I knew held a hidden sexual connotation. I shook my head in astonishment. Cornelius reminded me of a stealth bomber. I never heard him coming, but he always made a big impression on me before he left my sight. I took a long, deep breath and entered the library.

"Hello there, Ms. Starr," Harry greeted me as I entered the library.

"Hi, Mr. and Mrs. Turner. Please call me Lexie. What are the two of you reading?" I asked, making my voice pleasantly cordial.

"Well, Lexie, I've found this interesting biographical book about one of my all-time favorite groups, The Spice Girls," the sixty-something gentleman said, as he turned the book toward me to display a photo of Posh Spice, aka Victoria Beckham, singing into a microphone. "And Alma's looking through some tome regarding military strategies employed in World War Two. Very dry stuff, if you ask me, but Alma's intrigued with it for some reason. I guess it's due to her German background. Her family immigrated to America when she was very young."

German background or not, I couldn't imagine either one of them being interested in the book each had chosen, but I was continually amazed at the eccentricities of these Historical Society people.

"So, are you two doing okay? Considering what happened this morning and all? I know it had to be quite a shock to you. It certainly was to me."

"We're doing all right. But it was quite an unexpected turn of events, wasn't it?" Harry asked.

"Yes," I agreed. "Very much so."

"The investigators asked us to be ready to give a statement this afternoon, but neither of us heard or saw anything to report to them."

"Then that's what you should say in your statement."

"Have they come to any conclusions about who the perpetrator might be?" Harry spoke louder as his voice was nearly drowned out by a sound outside the library. We all looked up in time to catch a glimpse of Crystal through the glass doors. She was pushing a self-propelled vacuum sweeper down the hallway. She carried a feather duster in the other hand. I called out to her, and she looked startled. She must have been deep in thought. She waved off my offer to help her make up the guests' rooms for the very first time in her newly acquired position at the inn.

"It won't take me long," she said. "And I'll enjoy seeing how the suites are decorated, if the rest of the inn is any indication of the effort you and Stone put into finding and selecting furniture from the Victorian era."

"We scoured every antique store in the Midwest, or at least it feels as if we did. We were fortunate to find most of the paintings at the antique mall on Sycamore Street, right here in Rockdale. All but a few came from the same estate, the old Warrington home on Garnett Drive."

"Are the paintings in the parlor from the Warrington home? They're exquisite."

"Yes, and they should be exquisite," I said. "The paintings and artwork in the inn cost more than the furniture."

"I thought I recognized a few of them," Harry said, interrupting as he turned to his wife. "See? I was right. Remember when we dined at the Warringtons', years ago?"

Alma nodded and went back to reading. Crystal excused herself to continue down the hallway. I turned back to Harry as he repeated the question he'd asked earlier about whether or not a perpetrator had been identified.

"The investigation has barely begun, of course, and no suspects have been named yet. Do you or Alma have any thoughts about it at all? Do you know any reason why anyone might have wanted to see Mr. Prescott dead?"

"Could be just about anybody, I'd say."

"What do you mean?" I asked.

"Don't know a single soul who had any use for the man. Excuse my language, but he was a jackass, through and through. If I'd have thought I could get away with it, I might've considered knocking off Prescott myself."

"Good heavens, Harry! Mind what you say!" Alma finally spoke aloud, swatting her husband on the forearm with her book, which bore the likeness of Winston Churchill on its cover.

"Well, my dear, it happens to be true. And you know yourself, it's the God-awful truth."

"Well, maybe so, but we must not speak ill of the dead. You know better," Alma admonished her spouse with a look of indignation in her eyes. Then she lowered her voice to almost a whisper, and hissed, "And we needn't air our dirty laundry in public, either. Some things are just not meant to be shared."

Alma's last remarks were spoken as a definite warning. I caught it, and I'm sure Harry Turner did, too. I had a feeling he'd been about to tell me more about their previous dealings with the late Mr. Prescott, but now he'd been effectively squelched by his spouse. Harry looked at Alma in alarm, as if realizing what he'd almost disclosed, and then turned to me with an apprehensive expression on his lean, weathered face.

"I'm sorry, Lexie," he said. "Alma's right. I should be more respectful at a time like this. Not even a loathsome man like Horatio Prescott deserved a fate like the one he suffered. Alma and I both are very distressed by his untimely death."

Harry fell silent, and it was obvious I wouldn't be able to unearth any more information about the Turner's dirty laundry at this time, so I changed the subject. "Were either of you aware that Horatio was writing a book about restoring historic homes?"

"Oh, sure," Harry said. He seemed relieved to talk about something else. "We both were. It was common knowledge. I'd heard that just last week he'd received a call from his agent, who informed him he'd been offered a contract from a large publishing house. Otto Poffenbarger, who's penning a book about the same thing, was mad enough to spit. In fact, I think he did."

Harry chuckled at the recollection before he went on to say, "Otto's book would probably sell better as a cure for insomnia than anything else. I doubt his manuscript is chock full of scintillating facts and insights. Just more of the scientific drivel he spouts all the time."

"You don't like Mr. Poffenbarger?"

"Oh, Otto's a nice enough fellow, I suppose. He's just such a dry, boring person to converse with. I've had more interesting conversations with Tinkerbelle, my Persian cat, than I've had with Otto. I can almost understand why Patty rarely gives the man permission to speak. Or, Fatty Patty, I should say, as Horatio was known to call her."

"To her face?" I asked, in disbelief.

"Of course," he said. "He'd say it to intentionally provoke her."

"But why?"

"Who knows?" Harry shrugged. "Why did he do a lot of the things he did? Like I said, he was a jackass, through and through."

Alma swatted Harry with her book again, harder this time. I was beginning to think the guests with no motive to kill Mr. Prescott were few and far between. I had a lot to mull over and record in my notebook when I could find the time. The thought reminded me it was almost time to start preparing lunch.

I excused myself to assist Crystal in the kitchen. We'd be preparing spinach crepes, cream of asparagus soup, and chicken-salad finger sandwiches to serve to the guests for their mid-day meal. I could get some of the dishes prepared in advance while Crystal tackled the housekeeping chores. I figured it might take her a while because it was her first time to make up the rooms.

"I'd better get back to work. Don't you two get so involved in your reading you forget to come to the dining room for lunch in about half an hour," I said.

I knew I'd have to catch Harry alone in the next day or two and try to worm out the details of his animosity towards our "extinguished" guest, Horatio Prescott III. I was hearing a lot about laundry this morning, both clean and dirty, and I wanted to find out more about it!

"Mom?" I heard Wendy's anxious voice as Crystal gave the phone to me. She was calling from the County Coroner's office in St. Joseph, where she worked.

"Yeah, this is me."

"Are you and Stone okay?"

"Yes, honey, we're fine."

"They just hauled a body bag in here and told us the man had been killed at the Alexandria Inn. I couldn't believe it. What happened over there? Who killed him? Do you know? When did the murder occur? Did anyone witness it?" she asked. There was anxiety and concern in her voice as she rattled off questions.

"No, we don't know much yet. The victim's name is Horatio Prescott III, and he was to be inducted as the new president of the Rockdale Historical Society later on today. Stone and I found him dead in his room this morning. As I'm sure you know, he'd been shot in the back of the head. The Rockdale detectives are investigating the murder, but they don't know who killed him or why yet. Stone and I have decided to do a little investigating ourselves."

"Why does that not surprise me?" Wendy asked, dryly. "It was your idea, I suppose."

"Uh-huh."

"Figured so," Wendy said, with a hint of amusement in her tone. I could hear a buzzing sound in the background as Wendy spoke and wondered if Mr. Prescott's corpse was being sawed in half at that very moment. I felt a chill run up my spine and felt strangely relieved with Wendy's next statement. "By the way, Mom, later on today Nate is letting me perform the autopsy on this Prescott guy by myself since it is such a cut-and-dried case. He'll just be observing me as I work. It'll be my first time to fly solo, so to speak. I can hardly wait."

Nate Smith was the County Coroner, and he'd been training Wendy as his assistant for the last few months. He planned to retire in a few years and buy a waterfront condo in south Texas to live out his golden years. His wife had already retired from teaching at the secondary-education level.

Stone had encouraged Wendy to apply for the apprentice position with Nate when he'd heard through the local grapevine about the County Coroner's impending retirement. It'd be a longer drive for her than Kansas City, Kansas, but it'd be worth the inconvenience to have the chance to step into the coroner's position in two years. She'd have spent many years waiting for such an opportunity in Wyandotte County, Kansas, where she'd first gone to work, assisting a County Coroner who wasn't much older than she was.

On nights when she worked late or had to report to the coroner's lab early the following day, she could skip the long drive and stay overnight at the Alexandria Inn. She'd stayed at the inn often during the weeks Stone and I had worked day and night getting it ready for its grand opening. She'd helped out by spending her evenings with a sander or a paintbrush in her hand; working steadily while she rattled on about the cadaver she'd watched Nate Smith dissect that day. I had tried to concentrate on other, more pleasant things while nodding sporadically at Wendy's ramblings.

Eventually Wendy planned to buy a place of her own in St. Joseph or nearby Rockdale. She seemed confident I would end up selling my home in Shawnee and moving in with Stone at the Alexandria Inn. I had to admit I was already spending more time there with Stone than I was spending at my own home. Still, I hesitated to give up my independence entirely, despite the subtle hints by Stone and the gentle prodding by Wendy. But I set those thoughts aside to listen to Wendy chatter excitedly about her first "flying-solo" autopsy.

"Autopsy? I'm no expert, but I'd guess the bullet through his brain might have had something to do with the cause of his death," I said dryly.

"Duh," Wendy said with a laugh. "Good deduction, Mom.

However, you know it's customary to perform an autopsy in all homicide cases or whenever foul play is suspected. I could even be called on at a later date to testify in court, you know. I'm a bit nervous, but only because this is my very first time to handle the entire autopsy on my own. Oh, I hear Nate calling my name. I've got to get busy, Mom. Wish me luck."

"You've got it, honey. Call me at the inn this evening to let me know how the autopsy went, okay? There's some leftover lasagna in the fridge you can heat up for supper. I won't be home tonight. We've all been instructed to stay at the inn for the next couple of days—if possible, of course. With every guestroom filled, Stone needs me to help Crystal anyway. She's a pro, but even so, it's too much for one person to handle. Sometimes it's almost too much for the two of us to handle. These Historical Society people can be very demanding."

"Okay, I'll give you a call from home then. It'll be eight or nine, I'd imagine. Don't work too hard, Mom."

Crystal and I served pork roast with potatoes, carrots, and fried okra for supper, and now the guests were gathering in the parlor with their ever-present cups of coffee. The caffeine consumption was hitting a dangerous level, I feared. I was accustomed to drinking coffee from morning till night, but I wasn't sure about the guests.

While exiting the parlor with an empty carafe, I was fascinated by Cornelius Walker and Ernestine Fischer, who were dancing in the corner of the room. They were doing something resembling the fox trot, dancing in time to the music drifting out from the antique Atwater Kent radio on the fireplace mantel. For such an ordinary-looking man, Cornelius was an incredibly accomplished dancer, and Ernestine was doing all she could to keep up with him. I was compelled to stop and watch them from the doorway. Robert Fischer and Rosalinda

Swift were clapping along with the music, in appreciation of the show the dancers were putting on, and I joined in, applauding the pair enthusiastically at the conclusion of the song. I noticed, however, the lively beat of the music and the motion of the dancers had caused me to feel a little dizzy all of a sudden.

Back in the kitchen a few minutes later, I poured another pitcher of water into the coffeemaker and began working on the daunting pile of dirty dishes on the counter. I struggled with the task of washing them, feeling lethargic and slightly sick to my stomach. As I dried the last plate and was putting it back into the cabinet, the phone rang, and Crystal answered it after the first ring.

"It's for you," she said. "Your daughter."

"Thanks." I shut the cabinet door and hung the dishtowel up to dry.

"Are you all right?" Crystal asked as I stumbled, reaching for the phone. I nodded and gratefully sat down on the stool she slid across the floor toward me.

I greeted Wendy, who was calling from the coroner's lab again. She was excited about executing the autopsy on Horatio Prescott III without a single hitch. "As suspected, he was killed by a single gunshot wound to the head," she said. "I extracted a thirty-two-caliber slug from his skull, just behind the right eye socket."

Wendy said this in the same manner anyone else's daughter might when bragging about being named Employee of the Month. I found it a little distasteful.

"Surprise, surprise," I said. "Are you certain it wasn't something he ate? You know those chicken bones can be hazardous."

"What was unexpected though," Wendy continued, ignoring my sarcasm entirely, "was the damage we found to Mr.

Prescott's organs. Prior to being shot, he'd ingested some form of toxin."

"Ahh, so it *was* something he ate," I said, even as I realized I was being too glib. A man had been murdered, and I was making light of it. The giddiness was partially due to the almost intoxicated sensation I was suddenly experiencing.

"He hadn't ingested enough to kill him, but it's safe to say he wasn't feeling too whoopee this morning at the time he was murdered. There was also quite a bit of scotch in his system, so we think the poison might have been slipped into a drink and probably ingested just before midnight. I determined he died somewhere between four and six A.M., and Nate concurred with my conclusion."

"How could you determine the time of his death?"

"By the temperature of his liver. The liver also showed signs of degeneration from the presence of the poisonous substance."

"That would agree with the time I heard him hit the floor in the room above me, which was 5:08. What exactly is the poisonous substance found in his system?"

"Don't know yet," Wendy said, "but we should have the toxicology report back soon."

I tried to answer but began to cough as a result of a dry, burning throat that had been bothering me off and on all evening. I hacked again, and Wendy asked, "You okay, Mom? You haven't started smoking again, have you? You're coughing, and you just don't sound like yourself."

"No, honey, I haven't started smoking again, and I don't plan to. It's just a sore throat causing me to cough. It's nothing to worry about. I'm probably just catching a cold. Or it could just be the dry winter air in this place."

"Have you taken any Alka-Seltzer yet?" Wendy's answer to everything from a splinter to congestive heart failure was Alka-Seltzer. She swore Alka-Seltzer, if taken early enough, could ward off anything, whether it is a cold, the flu, or the black plague.

"No, not yet, but I'll check to see if Stone has any in his medicine cabinet. So, anyway, is it safe to assume Mr. Prescott was shot because the poison failed to do the trick?" I asked.

"That'd be my guess. No need to kill a guy twice."

After the Historical Society guests retired to their rooms for the evening, I joined Stone in the parlor to discuss the day's events. I had poured myself another cup of espresso and carried it in the room with me.

Stone gave me a long, tender kiss before he noticed the cup in my hand. "Good Lord, Lexie, are you still drinking coffee? Haven't you had more than enough of the stuff today already? You'll never get any sleep tonight."

"I gave up the prayer of sleeping a long time ago. But, actually, I'm feeling a bit nauseated at the moment, so I don't think I'd better drink anymore of this, anyway. I was just going to go check your medicine cabinet for Alka-Seltzer."

"I'll go buy a box of it for you if there isn't any in the cabinet. And maybe I'll pick up some Nyquil to help you sleep—so you won't be up all night."

"By the sounds of the floorboards creaking and groaning upstairs, I don't think I'll be the only person up all night. We went through a full three-pound can of coffee today, along with what was left from the other can we started with this morning."

"Got enough left for tomorrow?"

"No, but Crystal is going to pick some up on her way to work in the morning, along with a few other items we are running short on. We've got enough for several pots, which will get us started, at least."

"Good. Crystal's been a real asset to us, hasn't she? Can you make sure she's reimbursed for whatever she has to purchase?

I'll make sure she gets a bonus when this is all over with, too."

I assured him I'd take care of reimbursing Crystal, and then told him everything I'd learned throughout the day, none of which I'd found time to jot down in my notebook. He listened intently, as he always did. He then placed his index finger under my chin and lifted my face to study it with scrutiny. "You look flushed, sweetheart. I don't want you working as long or hard tomorrow, you hear? These people are not invalids; they can fend for themselves tomorrow if Crystal is not available to wait on them. Crystal doesn't have to be at their beck and call either, for that matter."

I nodded, too tired to argue. I was feeling nauseated again, more and more like I might upchuck what little pork roast and potatoes I'd managed to eat earlier. I tried to direct my attention away from the queasiness in my stomach to Stone as he spoke about his day.

He told me he'd been tied up with the investigators much of the day, and other than Robert Fischer, he'd only had time to chat with Cornelius Walker. And even then it was just for a few minutes before supper he'd been able to talk to him.

Stone discovered that, several decades ago, Cornelius had been engaged to Horatio's first wife, Ethel. According to Cornelius, lies and deception utilized by Mr. Prescott had allowed Ethel to be stolen from him. According to Cornelius, Prescott had convinced Ethel her fiancé was of questionable character, and marriage to him was sure to cause her great heartache. Ethel had dumped Cornelius and soon found herself engaged to Horatio. Cornelius had never married, or even become engaged again in the wake of his sorrow at losing the "love of his life." He was further devastated when Ethel died mysteriously in a boating accident on the day before she would have celebrated her and Horatio's tenth anniversary.

Horatio, however, was apparently less distraught following

Ethel's untimely death. He remarried within three months of the tragedy, to a woman who was fifteen years his junior. Several years later, his second wife also died prematurely, in a horrific house fire, which was eventually determined to have been set by an unknown arsonist.

"How awful," I said. "Mr. Prescott sure had to endure a lot of tragedies, didn't he?"

"I don't know about Mr. Prescott, but those close to him sure did."

I caught Stone's meaning but wondered why he thought Horatio Prescott might have been responsible for the deaths of his two former wives. I was going to ask him about this when I suddenly felt a sharp, stabbing pain in my abdomen, just seconds before a veil of darkness settled over me and I crumpled into an undignified heap on the kitchen floor.

CHAPTER SIX

The next thing I remember was opening my eyes and being startled by two other pairs of eyes, worried and inquisitive, staring down at me. I glanced around quickly and discovered I was lying on a hospital bed. There was a sedative-type medication and a bag of saline solution dripping into my arm via an IV tube, an oxygen monitor clipped to my index finger, and a heart monitor beeping to the side of my bed.

"Mom?" I heard Wendy ask in a concerned voice. "Can you hear me?"

"Yes," I tried to answer, but my throat was raw and swollen.

"Don't try to talk, honey." Stone's voice was soothing. He had an apologetic tone to his voice as he said, "They've just had to pump your stomach."

"What happened?" I asked. My words were raspy. I sounded like an old metal gate rubbing against a wooden fence post.

"They discovered traces of tansy oil in your system, Mom," Wendy said. "It's the same toxic poison we found in Prescott, according to the results of the toxicology report."

"Tansy oil?" I'd never heard of it.

"Uh-huh. According to Nate, tansy is a poisonous herb once considered a 'cure-all.' Less than a tablespoon of the oil derived from it can be deadly. In other words, Mom, someone tried to kill you. And it looks like it was the same person who killed Horatio Prescott."

"Fortunately," Stone said, shaking his head as if he couldn't believe his own words, "the massive amount of coffee you drank today probably saved your life. It diluted the tansy oil enough to prevent it from being a lethal dose."

I nodded. My throat was too sore to speak more than a few words at a time. Stone spooned a few ice chips into my mouth, giving me immediate relief.

Wendy lifted my hand up to inspect the IV infusion site. "Good, no signs of bruising," she said. She turned toward Stone as she spoke again. "Why would anyone want to kill both Mr. Prescott and Mom? It's not as if they have anything in common. Do you think the person has a vendetta against the Alexandria Inn for some reason? Could any other guests be in danger?"

Stone considered my daughter's questions for a moment before shaking his head. He brushed loose tendrils of hair away from his forehead. "It's possible, I guess," he said, "but I don't think it's very likely, Wendy. I expect it's more probable the killer is concerned that your mother may stumble on to the truth of who's responsible for the murder. She's been questioning all the Historical Society guests, and it appears as if it is one of them, not an outsider, who's responsible for the murder. That's why I don't want her questioning any of them anymore. I don't want her to even be present at the inn until the perpetrator is in police custody. The success of the inn is nowhere near worth her getting injured or killed over."

Wendy nodded in complete agreement with Stone. I felt slightly betrayed. The ice chips had soothed and moistened my throat so I could now speak clearly. I'm sure I sounded more annoyed than I meant to, considering both of them had my best interests at heart. "I refuse to back down, Stone. I'll be more cautious, but I won't let the killer intimidate me."

Stone knew me well enough by now to know I meant exactly what I said. Being poisoned by the perpetrator only increased my resolve to help see him ferreted out and arrested. Stone sighed and dropped his head into his hands. I listened to the near-hysterical ranting of my daughter, while sucking on a throat lozenge Stone had given me.

When Wendy finally settled down and came to the same resigned realization as Stone, I cleared my throat and said, "I recall having set my cup down on the sofa table while I gathered up the ashtrays to empty and rinse out. Boris is the only guest who smokes, but he seems intent on distributing his ashes evenly among all the ashtrays in the various rooms. With the guests milling around in the parlor, any one of them could have slipped a dose of tansy oil in my coffee undetected."

I paused a moment to reflect. "Weren't there ashes in the ashtray in Horatio's room this morning?" I asked. "I remember thinking the ashtray needed to be cleaned. That seems odd because I don't think Horatio was a smoker."

"I don't remember even looking at the ashtray, but it wouldn't have been my primary concern at the time. Nor do I remember if Horatio smoked," Stone said. "But I don't really recall ever seeing him with a cigarette or cigar, or even a pipe."

I couldn't remember seeing him with a cigarette or cigar either, and I tended to notice that kind of thing even more since I quit smoking. I always had to remind myself to keep my mouth shut because there was nothing more annoying than an ex-smoker expounding on the stupidity of smoking.

I wondered who, beside Boris, could have deposited ashes in Horatio's ashtray. I was trying to think back to earlier in the evening and visualize exactly what had happened and in exactly what sequence. I was having trouble thinking through the fog filtering into my mind. The medication dripping into my IV tube was beginning to take effect.

"I also remember the coffee took on a bitter taste after I

retrieved the cup from the sofa table," I said, after a lengthy interval.

"And you continued to drink it?" Wendy asked incredulously.

"Yes, I did—out of habit, I suppose. I was distracted by other things at the time and attributed the unusual taste to the fact I'd been drinking so much of the stuff all day long. Strong coffee can be a mite bitter all on its own, you know."

Wendy and Stone were both looking at me as if I were one goose short of a gaggle, so I decided to lie back down to rest for a moment. In my current condition, it took too much effort to try to convince them I was not losing my mind. I closed my heavy eyelids and swallowed the melted ice accumulating in the back of my throat. Stone squeezed behind the hospital bed and began to knead the taut muscles in my neck and shoulders.

"Who could feel threatened enough by my simple questioning to attempt to kill me?" I asked. Neither Stone nor Wendy replied, so I wasn't sure I'd even asked the question out loud. I was feeling more and more relaxed from the medicine and from the hypnotizing feel of Stone's hand rubbing the tension out of my upper body.

Could it be a guest I hadn't found the time to question yet? I wondered. Maybe someone who didn't want to be questioned by a nosy, interfering servant? It was my last conscious thought before I fell into a deep, dreamless sleep.

CHAPTER SEVEN

I was released from the hospital at about noon on Tuesday. I left with a long list of instructions that included returning to the ER if any of my symptoms worsened or if any new ones developed.

As the male nurse wheeled me to the front vestibule, Stone walked along beside the wheelchair carrying my coat and fanny pack. He'd arrived at the hospital just as I was signing the release form.

"Anything new?" I asked.

"A few things," he said. "I'll bring you up to date on the way back to the inn."

I knew Stone didn't want to say anything in the presence of the nurse, so I changed the subject to something more mundane. The weather was always a good subject when one wanted to make idle chatter. "Snow's all gone, I see. I hope yesterday's snowfall was winter's last gasp and spring is just around the corner. Maybe this was the last major winter storm we'll have this season."

"Could be, but I doubt it. More snow is predicted for tonight. Quite a lot of it, they're now predicting. The forecast gets more intimidating every time the weatherman revises it."

After assisting me as I climbed into the passenger seat of a silver Chevy Cavalier, Stone took his place behind the steering wheel and prepared to drive the car out of the parking lot.

"I borrowed Tony's car," he said, as he turned toward me to help me fasten my seat belt. "My car is at the dealership getting an oil change and a tune-up, and your Jeep's gas gauge was on empty. I will fill up for you this afternoon."

"Thanks! Who's Tony?"

"Oh, you know. The Italian-looking guy on the remodeling crew with the ponytail and earring. He's the one who promised to take me crappie fishing at Perry Lake this spring."

"Oh, sure. He's the painter. I'd forgotten his name was Tony. I think he looks Italian because he *is* Italian. His last name is Morelli, if I remember right. He told me his grandparents still live in Sicily. Anyway, it was nice of him to loan you his car and thoughtful of you to ask him if you could borrow it."

"I wanted to make sure you'd be comfortable."

"I'm quite comfortable, thanks. I'll be completely recuperated shortly. I feel almost like my old self today."

"Good. But you need to rest and take it easy for a while anyway. You scared at least ten years off my life when you passed out in the kitchen last night."

"I'm sorry—"

"It's not your fault, honey. And I'm glad you got a good night's sleep. It's more than I can say for any of the rest of us."

"Why? Did something else happen?" I asked as he braked the car to a stop at a red light.

"No, thank God. Prescott's murder and the attempt on your life were enough as it was. I just think our guests were afraid to go to sleep last night, lest the same thing happen to them that felled Mr. Prescott. There were people scurrying about all night long, from one room to the next. I had no less than a dozen reports of suspicious sounds and intruder sightings. The guests were all carrying weapons of varying degrees of effectiveness, from Rosalinda's pepper spray to Cornelius's golf club. And Robert Fischer whacked Patty Poffenbarger on the head with his pipe when she surprised him as she was sneaking out of the kitchen with a snack. She has an under-active thyroid, you know."

"Yes, of course," I said with a laugh. "I'll bet Patty had a thing or two to say about the indignity she suffered. 'Peckish Patty Poffenbarger pissed when painfully popped with pipe while packing pillaged pastries from pantry to parlor.' How's that for a tongue twister?"

"Pretty pathetic, my perky partner," Stone said in amusement. "But I admit I couldn't say it three times in a row. Are you sure you're feeling okay, honey?"

"Sorry, Stone. I know I sound half crazy, but I'm just so relieved to be on my way back to the inn. I don't like hospitals very much."

"I can understand that. But I can't help worrying about you," Stone said, patting my hand, which was resting on my knee. "You're right about Patty, though. She's pissed and still spouting off about an impending lawsuit, I'm sure. It was a long night, I assure you. I missed you more than I can say."

Stone reached over again and rubbed the top of my thigh for a few seconds and then placed his right hand back on the steering wheel. His forehead appeared to have several new furrows etched in to it.

"I missed you, too," I said. "So what's going on at the inn today?"

"Not much so far. It's been pretty quiet this morning. Boris Dack left for his office at about seven this morning and told the investigators he'd return by eleven. I just spoke with Crystal on my cell phone, and Boris has still not arrived back at the inn. I thought we might drive by the D&P Enterprise office building. Harry Turner, rather reluctantly, it seemed to me, explained where the building was located. Sound okay to you? We can head straight back to the inn, if you'd rather," Stone said.

"No, I'd like to see the building, and it'd be a good time to do it, while we're driving a less conspicuous vehicle—one that doesn't stand out like my yellow Jeep or your red Corvette."

"Yes, that's what I thought. This silver car blends in well. It seems to me as if every other vehicle on the road these days is putrid or silver—"

"Putrid?"

"Excuse me, I meant pewter. It's beautiful, I'll admit, but it's become such a popular color for vehicles, I'm getting sick of seeing it. Does the sign ahead say Executive Drive? I can't read it from here."

I couldn't either, so I found my glasses in my fanny pack and slipped them on. I saw the sign read Executive Drive just as Stone made a quick left turn onto the street.

"That building on the right says D&P Enterprises on its front," I said, pointing to a modern, three-story chrome and glass structure. Stone slowed down and steered Tony's Chevy into the nearly vacant parking lot. A white cardboard sign was tacked on the front door of the building. Stone pulled the car up to the door and stepped out to read the sign printed with a red magic marker. He re-entered the car, shivered dramatically, and turned toward me.

"Chilly out there, isn't it?" he commented, placing his icy fingers against my neck. He then pulled them back and began blowing on his hands to warm them. "The sign says the business will be temporarily closed due to the unexpected death of Horatio Prescott. Employees will be notified by phone when they're to return to work. Looking through the glass doors, though, I saw a man who looked like Boris going out the back door with a very large, bulging trash bag. I'm almost positive it was Boris, even though I didn't see his blue Chrysler in the front parking lot. Now I'm going to sneak around to the back of the building and see if I can see anything else."

I waited while Stone walked around to the back of the building. While he was gone, I saw Boris pull around the building in his navy blue sedan. He drove out of the parking lot without even glancing my way. Just a few seconds later I heard the trunk on Tony's Chevy pop open behind me. I turned to look at Stone as he tossed a large trash sack in the trunk and then jumped back into the car.

"I want to follow him. Which way did he turn?" he asked, gasping for breath. I pointed south, and Stone drove out of the parking lot and turned in that direction. "Boy, am I winded! Next time I buy a stationary bike I'm going to use it more than a half dozen times before I sell it in a garage sale for five bucks."

"You used a stationary bike six times?" I asked. "I'm impressed. I can't remember using mine more than twice. But I got ten bucks for it because it was still in 'like new' condition. I hadn't even removed the original price sticker, yet."

"Yes, but did you dust yours for three years before you sold it?"

"No, I disposed of it quickly because I didn't want to be reminded of my vow to get in shape and use it an hour a day, every day. It sat in the corner of the living room and taunted me for just two months before I sold it."

"Good for you. I love a woman who can stand up to a piece of exercise equipment and show it she's the boss."

I chuckled at his remark. It struck me at that moment I had laughed more in the few months I'd known Stone than I'd laughed in the entire twenty years since my husband Chester had died. Having a man in my life again was turning out to be good for me in more ways than I'd anticipated. "What's in the bag, Stone? Any idea?"

"No, other than what appears to be a lot of shredded paper. Later we'll check out the contents of the trash bag. He was sure intent on getting rid of it in the dumpster. I could see by the look on his face he was convinced no one had seen him take that bag out of the building. He's covering his butt for some reason—getting rid of a paper trail or evidence of something. He's either guilty of murdering his business partner, or concerned about white-collar crimes that might be uncovered in an all-out investigation. That'd be my bet at this point."

We soon caught up with the dark blue Chrysler Concorde. Stone tried to stay several cars behind Boris. We followed him for about twenty miles before he turned off into the immense parking lot of the new horseracing facility. The racetrack had caused a lot of controversy among local residents as it was being built. The newspapers had been full of editorials for and against the new racetrack. Many of the town's citizens thought all the new casinos in the Kansas City area were detrimental enough without adding other outlets for gambling.

I had to agree the new gaming establishments could prove to be the downfall of many people with a weakness for gambling. Not only an addicted gambler, but also almost anyone under the right circumstances, could be enticed to bet their entire house payment on a chance to win a large jackpot. And, like it or not, the odds are never in the gambler's favor. On many occasions, even I had been known to donate more money than I'd intended at the casinos. I had an unrequited love for the triple diamond slot machines for several years. I finally got tired of losing all the money I took with me.

"Hmm. I wonder what he's doing here," Stone said, bringing me out of my reverie on the pitfalls of the area's casinos. "I'm going to go in there and see if I can learn anything without being seen by Boris. If he spots me, I'll just walk up to the betting cage and place a twenty dollar bet on the number three horse to win, nod at Boris if I catch his eye, and leave. You stay in the car, out of the cold wind. I won't be long. I'll leave the motor running and the heater on for you."

I would have liked to go with him, but I didn't really feel all that strong yet, so I nodded and said, "Okay, take your time. And make it horse number one. I think having the inside rail is a definite advantage in any horse race."

Stone looked at me in amazement and nodded. Then he reached into the back seat and picked up a red K.C. Chiefs ball cap belonging to Tony, and put on a pair of sporty, wrap-around, sunglasses lying on the dash. Stone never wore a hat, and I had to admit just the addition of a ball cap and glasses made him difficult to recognize. The cap hid his attractive silver hair and made him look a bit goofy.

I suppose it was no more than fifteen to twenty minutes later when Stone returned to the car, although it seemed much longer. I'd almost dozed off when I heard Stone's key in the door. He hopped in the car and flung the ball cap to the back seat. He kept the sunglasses on as he shifted the car into reverse. He was unusually animated and expectant. I knew he was becoming more and more intrigued with our sleuthing mission. I was, too. It was more involved than I would've guessed at the beginning.

"What did you find out?" I asked, anxious to share in his excitement.

"Well, it appears that Boris has a gambling problem, and some significant unpaid gambling debts. I was standing behind a concrete pillar when Boris walked out of the men's restroom. A large, muscular guy who looked as if he could easily bend crowbars in half with his bare hands immediately approached him. Neither one had a clue I was standing behind the pillar and could hear their entire conversation. The big, burly guy asked Boris if he had 'the money,' and Boris told him he didn't, but he would have it within the week. Then the guy told him if he didn't have the money his boss was owed by Saturday, Boris could look forward to having his face rearranged."

"Oh, my! I take it this big, muscular guy is a loan shark?"

"Well, he's a goon for the loan shark, anyway. Boris promised to have the money because he had an inside tip on a bet he was about to make. He said Willie's White Lightning was a shoe-in. The goon didn't look too impressed, but Boris was so emphatic about it, I was almost tempted to bet a hundred bucks on Willie's White Lightning, myself. After the goon walked away, Boris made a call on his cell phone and practically hissed when he spoke into it. 'Where are those damn birds? I need the money, now!' I heard him say into the phone."

"Damn birds?" I asked.

"That's what he said. Damn birds. I'm sure of it. Then Boris told Shorty, the caller, he'd be in his room at the inn at six o'clock this evening awaiting a call, and if Shorty didn't come through with some positive news about the birds, his ass was going to be grass."

"And Boris would be the lawnmower, no doubt?"

"No doubt."

"I wonder who this Shorty guy is and what Boris meant by the 'damn birds.' What can birds have to do with anything?" I asked.

"No way to tell."

"Maybe there is, Stone. If we can somehow get Boris's cell phone, we can check his log of outgoing calls. See what phone number he called at about one o'clock today and call it ourselves to see who answers. Or, if that doesn't work, we might be able to do a cross-check on the computer to see who the phone number belongs to."

"Good idea, Lexie," Stone said. I smiled as he cleared his throat and continued, "For someone who used to be opposed to the very idea of owning a cell phone, you seem to be quite familiar with the things now."

"I've learned they really are very handy and useful, if not downright critical at times. I love my new Nokia phone," I

74

admitted. "I don't know how we all got by without them for so long."

"Me either. I still need to look for a different phone carrier, though. One that gets a stronger signal here in Rockdale than my current carrier. The service I used in Myrtle Beach doesn't seem to fare well here in the Midwest. It seems like I'm on analog roam most of the time."

"I'll bet that gets expensive in a hurry."

"Uh-huh, it sure does. Hey, are you hungry? While the investigators are at the inn taking the last couple of statements, we could stop and get some lunch at the Corner Café," Stone suggested.

"Yes, let's do. I'm starving. I was served a full breakfast at the hospital, but I didn't recognize anything on my tray, so I hesitated to eat any of it. I drank the coffee, of course—"

"Of course."

"—and ate one slice of cold, soggy toast."

When we finished eating our bowls of vegetable-beef soup with crackers, we left the café and climbed back into Tony's car. Stone started the engine in order to turn on the heater, and then dialed the inn on his cell phone. After numerous rings, Cornelius Walker finally answered the phone.

"Hello, Cornelius, is Crystal there?" Stone asked.

"Yes, I'm sure she is. I just saw her a while ago," Cornelius said. From the passenger seat I could plainly hear his nasal voice over the phone. "I'm not sure where the delectable young angel in an apron is at the moment, however. Would you like me to go find her for you? Tracking down beautiful women is my forte."

"No, no, that's fine, Cornelius," Stone said, laughing at Cornelius's remark. "Do you know if Boris Dack has returned to the inn yet? He had expected to return around eleven."

"I think he's just arriving now, as a matter of fact. I see a blue car pulling up the drive. It looks like his Chrysler Concorde. Do you want me to go outside and bring him to the phone?"

"No, that's not necessary. We'll be back to the inn shortly, anyway. Oh, but Cornelius, you could do me a favor. I need you to tell Crystal we're going to be stopping at the store to get some chicken, rice, and zucchini for tonight. Lexie will help Crystal fry the chicken. Crystal expressed a concern this morning about what she was going to prepare and serve for supper."

"Okay, fried chicken does sound good. I'll tell her as soon as I see her again," Cornelius said.

"Are you sure you won't get side-tracked and forget?"

"I'll remember. I promise. I do have a pornographic memory, you know."

CHAPTER EIGHT

Detective Wyatt Johnston was sitting at the kitchen table when we arrived at the inn. He'd helped himself to a cup of coffee while chatting with Crystal as she cleaned up the lunchtime dishes. She'd just finished serving a simple mid-day meal of sandwiches and fruit salad. The leftovers from the meal were spread out on the table in front of the officer. Detective Johnston was eyeing the food in anticipation, like a buzzard bearing down on road kill.

He gave me a questioning look as he motioned toward the platter of leftover sandwiches. "May I?" he asked, as I unloaded the groceries from the paper sacks and placed them on the marble counter for Crystal to stash away in the pantry.

"Sure, help yourself, Detective. Whatever you or the other officers don't eat will go to waste. Stone and I stopped for lunch on the way home, and everyone else has already eaten, as well. Help yourself to some fruit salad, too."

I wasn't surprised when he ignored the last offer. Detective Johnston didn't strike me as a fruit salad type of guy. I was amazed seconds later, when the detective selected a turkey and tomato sandwich and then devoured nearly half of it in one bite.

After the officer had polished off the rest of the sandwich with two more bites, he sorted through the remaining leftovers for another. This time he chose a ham and cheese. While he ate the second sandwich, Stone pitched the bag of trash down the basement stairs. He didn't mention to the detective how he'd obtained the bag or where it had come from. I'm sure if Wyatt Johnston was aware of anything other than the sandwich he was inhaling, he only assumed it was trash originating at the inn. After Johnston finished eating a third and last sandwich and had wiped his hands on the legs of his slacks, Stone asked, "What's up, Wyatt?"

"Right now, Ron and Orion have the black light set up upstairs, testing your guests' hands for gunshot residue. I just came from up there, and they were down to the last couple of guests. No sign of the residue has been found yet, by the way. Assuming none is found on the last two guests, the Poffenbargers, we'll probably release all of them to return to their homes tomorrow morning. Not that we're formally holding them here to begin with. I'm sure you'll both be glad to see them all leave, though."

"Is there any particular reason for the gunshot residue testing?" Stone asked. "Are there new developments indicating one of our guests is responsible for the shooting?"

"Not really," Wyatt said. "The residue test is just a formality, and probably all for naught, anyway." Wyatt continued talking, although neither Stone nor I had reacted or responded to his remark about being glad to see the guests leave. "The sergeant is across town right now, arresting a man named Randall on first-degree murder charges."

"Randall?" I asked. The name was not familiar to me.

"Yeah, Peter Randall. They've got him on probable cause, I guess. According to Sergeant O'Brien, there's a history of bad blood between Prescott and Randall. Randall used to be Prescott's personal stockbroker and financial advisor. Some investments Randall recommended a few months ago went south and caused a big fracas between the two men. Prescott lost a ton of money and filed a lawsuit against Randall on fraudulent practices."

"Didn't Randall have an alibi for his whereabouts Sunday night and early Monday morning?" Stone asked.

"No. At least not one that could be corroborated by anyone. He said he went to the old movie theatre downtown, the one that plays old classics at midnight every night for two bucks a ticket. It's right across the street from Randall's house, as a matter of fact. His photo was shown to all the employees at the theatre, and not one of them recognized Randall or remembered him being there Sunday night. They showed the movie, *Oh, God!*, that night, and when asked who played the part of God, Randall stated he couldn't recall."

"He sat through the whole movie and couldn't remember that George Burns played God?" Stone asked.

"That's just it. He said he stayed until the movie theatre closed just after two A.M., and yet he couldn't come up with John Denver's name, either. He told the detectives he slept through most of the movie. Yeah, right. Sure he did!"

"Hmm, sounds suspicious, doesn't it?" Stone said, with a shake of his head. "But, it's doesn't exactly make him a murderer. Is that all the investigators have to go on? It seems a little weak to me. I've fallen asleep in movie theatres on numerous occasions, myself. Haven't you?"

"Yeah, once or twice, I guess," the detective said. "For now, that's all they have on the guy, but they feel like they've got the right man pinned as Prescott's killer. Now they'll work to build a case around Peter Randall."

I had doubts that Peter Randall was the killer, and obviously Stone did as well. I knew the Rockdale Police Department had limited resources and was not often called upon to investigate a homicide, but the idea of throwing a dart at a wall full of balloons, blindfolded, and building a case around whatever random name was behind a broken balloon, did not sit well with me. It seemed like incredibly lazy detective work. There had to be a lot of innocent people rotting away in prison cells for that very reason. In this instance, there were too many people with motives to kill Horatio Prescott—motives just as strong and compelling as Peter Randall's—and the police should be expanding the circle of suspects and running down all sorts of clues and leads. Each guest at the inn should be closely evaluated, for it seemed to me each had a reason to dislike the victim as much as Peter Randall disliked him.

I knew I'd sat through many movies that, later on, I couldn't have made one intelligent comment about. And I had slept through Tom Hanks's movie *Castaway* not once, but twice, in the same week. Some people, like me, were just not movie aficionados and didn't know one actor from another. It would never have occurred to me that something so insignificant could cause a person to find himself in front of a jury, possibly facing the death penalty for a murder he hadn't committed.

"What about the footprints in the snow? The prints they found seem to come from someone inside the inn, and there was no sign of intruders or a forced entry. Has the investigating team cleared all the guests here at the inn?" I asked Wyatt Johnston.

"I don't think they ever really did much scrutinizing of the Historical Society members, other than the customary fingerprinting, gunshot residue checking, and routine questioning. I do know they considered the footprints as *non sequitur* material, of no particular significance to the investigation," Wyatt said.

"I'm not sure I agree, but they're the experts. I'm just a library assistant. Anything else new?"

"Umm, well, let's see. I did hear Veronica was notified about the death of her father. She's flying into town this afternoon. It's rumored she's considering the idea of hiring a P.I. on her own. Some hotshot private eye she knows from Camdenton, down around the Lake of the Ozarks. Veronica doesn't put much faith in my department's ability to solve the murder case, I guess."

I wasn't sure I did either, and I couldn't blame Veronica for bringing in her own private investigator. In her shoes, I would have done the same thing. There didn't seem to be an overabundance of effort on the part of the Rockdale Police Department. They were efficient and knowledgeable, but seemed a bit lackluster in their objective of making sure that justice was served—almost as if any suspect would suffice, regardless of his guilt or innocence.

"One thing's clear," the detective said. "There's no evidence the victim put up any kind of resistance. So chances are he either knew his assailant or he was taken completely by surprise." Or possibly both, I thought.

While I was cutting up the whole fryers we'd purchased, Stone came into the kitchen to check on me. He didn't want me overdoing it, as he'd repeated on several occasions. I finished whacking the chicken up into pieces and reached into the fridge for the zucchini to clean and slice. Stone took the bag from me and handed it over to Crystal, who'd just entered the room and indicated she wanted to prepare the produce. "I can handle it, Lexie. You rest," she said, taking the knife and bag of zucchini squash from Stone.

Stone held my hand and led me from the kitchen down to the basement to show me a few of the things he'd discovered in the trash bag he'd confiscated from D&P's dumpster. Most of the bag's contents had been through a shredder, but a few pieces of paper had been wadded up and thrown away intact, as if someone was in a hurry to dispose of them. Stone was just beginning to sort through those papers. "Check this one out," he said, handing me a sheet of paper after he smoothed it out with his hand.

I glanced at the official-looking document, scanning it hurriedly. It was a consent form, written on D&P Enterprise's letterhead. It allowed only representatives of the Arnold Accounting Firm to have access to D&P Enterprise's account information. At the bottom of the form there was the phone number of the accounting firm, and the signatures of both Horatio Prescott and Boris Dack.

"Hmm, I wonder."

"You wonder what?" Stone asked.

"Don't know if anything will come of it, but I have an idea."

"I was afraid you might," Stone said after a long drawn-out sigh.

"Relax. Nothing dangerous is involved."

I unclipped my cell phone from my waistband and called the phone number on the paper while Stone watched me with a curious expression. I had no idea what I was going to say, so decided to play it by ear.

"Arnold Accounting." I heard the female voice of a young woman, sounding quite bored.

"Hello. This is Wilma from Rockdale Bank and Trust. I need to speak to the accountant in charge of the D&P Enterprise account," I said.

"I don't know who'd that be," the young woman replied. I could almost see her filing her nails as she spoke into the phone. "Let me forward you to the owner, Mary. Please hold."

I listened to elevator music for several minutes before Mary came on the line. "This is Mary Arnold, may I help you?"

"Um, yes, Ms. Arnold. This is Wilma from Rockdale Bank and Trust. I need to speak to the person in charge of the D&P Enterprise account."

"Actually, D&P's a large contract and there are several accountants assigned to their account. We've just heard from one of our other clients that Mr. Prescott has died. Do you know if that's true?"

"Yes, ma'am, I'm afraid it is. Mr. Prescott suffered an unfortunate and untimely death early yesterday morning. All of us here at the bank are very saddened by the news. That's what has precipitated this call, as a matter of fact. Because of Mr. Prescott's sudden death, we've been notified there will be a thorough investigation into his finances, and the finances of his business. Have you personally been involved in the D&P Enterprises account at all, Mary? Have you, by any chance, dealt with anyone here at Rockdale Bank and Trust on D&P's account?"

"No, not personally. I'm ashamed to admit I've never even been inside your bank. But, although I've never met him in person, there have been a couple of instances where I've spoken on the phone with Mr. Myers, the president of your bank, on behalf of D&P Enterprises. Mr. Myers's son, Chad, just happens to be one of my son's best friends," Ms. Arnold said.

"Chad's a good kid, isn't he?" I asked, as if I'd known Mr. Myers's son since the day he was born.

"Uh, yeah, he's a good kid," she answered, with a touch of amusement in her voice. "Anyway, I assign accounts to my employees and am seldom personally involved beyond that. Could I forward you to one of the accountants who handles the contract?" Mary Arnold asked.

I'd found out what I needed to know. "No, that's okay. Mainly we just wanted to inform you one of the partners of the company had passed."

"Thank you," Mary said, with a touch of sadness in her voice.

"No, thank you," I said softly.

After telling him I'd be back to the inn in less than an hour, I left Stone, who was still sorting through the trash. I changed into a dressier outfit, put on a coat, and drove my Jeep to the Rockdale Bank and Trust. I parked in one of the customer parking spots, dabbed a little ChapStick on my dry lips, and strolled into the bank.

Inside, I told one of the tellers I needed to speak with Mr. Myers, the bank's president. She asked me to have a seat and informed me Mr. Myers would be with me in a few minutes. I sat and sifted through issues of *Money* and *Business Week* magazines for about ten minutes before I was called back into Mr. Myers's office.

"Good afternoon, Mr. Myers. I've spoken with you several times on the phone but have never had the privilege of meeting you in person," I said cordially. "I'm Mary Arnold of Arnold Accounting. You know, Chad's friend's mother."

"Oh, but of course. You sound different in person than you do on the phone, Mary. Do you have a cold?"

"Yes, as a matter of fact, I do." I smiled, sniffed dramatically, and then added, "I think I'm past the contagious stage, however."

"Don't worry about passing it on to me. My entire family is just getting over it, so I'm probably already immune. Have a seat."

"Thanks."

"It's nice to finally meet you, Ms. Arnold. Your son is a fine man. I just spoke with him at a benefit dinner this last weekend," Mr. Myers said. "I certainly would not have expected Roger's mother to be so young. What can I do for you today?"

Whoops, I hadn't taken Chad and Roger's ages into consideration. I'd just assumed that the two "sons" were of school age, maybe ten or eleven, rather than grown men. Now I was sure Mr. Myers was wondering if I'd become pregnant in the fifth grade.

"Thank you. I guess I did marry fairly young. And I assure

you I'm older than you may think. The reason I'm here, however, is to inform you one of your clients, Mr. Prescott, of D&P Enterprises has suddenly passed."

"Horatio?" Mr. Myers asked. He was obviously stunned by the news. "How dreadful. He's been banking here for ages. What happened? Heart attack?"

"No, Mr. Prescott was shot. Murdered, I regret to say. The homicide case is currently under investigation by the Rockdale Police Department. It's not clear yet who the perpetrator might be, but they're following several leads, and they already have a suspect in custody."

"Oh, how dreadful. Is the suspect anyone I might know?" Mr. Myers asked.

"He's a financial consultant named Peter Randall."

"Peter Randall? No, not Pete. No, I just can't see Pete murdering anyone." Mr. Myers shook his head, a scowl on his face.

"I've never met the man."

"I have, and I believe they've pointed the finger at the wrong person. Peter would never . . . well, whatever. That's none of my business, and I guess the police know what they're doing. It's quite dreadful, anyway," Mr. Myers repeated. Although he expressed surprise at the mention of Peter Randall as a suspect, I sensed he didn't seem completely shocked about the fact someone would want to kill Horatio. "How I can I be of help?" he asked.

"Because of the situation, the company's finances need to be scrutinized and audited. I'm sure you can understand the need for that," I said. I laid the signed consent form down on Mr. Myers's desk. "I just need to pick up the particulars on D&P Enterprises so we can begin the lengthy process. There's no reason to delay something that's going to have to be handled in the near future, anyway. If you could just photocopy the last few months' worth of statements for me, I'd appreciate it. Three months should be sufficient. You can keep the original copies here at the bank."

"Certainly, Ms. Arnold. I'll get the files for you. It will just take a few minutes to run Xerox copies of all the account statements. There are a number of them, you know."

"Yes, of course," I said with an understanding nod.

"I'll have my secretary bring you a cup of coffee, if you'd like."

"Thank you, I could use a cup. It will soothe my raw throat."

"How do you take it?" Mr. Myers asked in a cordial tone.

"Black, please."

"Fine, I'll tell her and be back with the information on the account in just a few minutes. I sure do regret to hear about Mr. Prescott's demise, Mary. He wasn't exactly one of my favorite clients, but nonetheless, I don't like to hear he was murdered."

Why did this revelation not surprise me? I didn't think Horatio Prescott was on anyone's list of favorite people.

CHAPTER NINE

I arrived at the inn in less than half an hour. Driving back, I wondered if I shouldn't drop off the account information at Arnold Accounting after I studied it. I'm sure the way I obtained it wasn't entirely legal. If I dropped it off in a plain manila envelope, perhaps no one would question how it got there. With any luck at all, Mr. Myers and Mary Arnold would never have an occasion to meet in person; for then, Myers would realize he'd been duped. Rockdale was a small town; we were bound to run into each other again sometime in the future. But I would deal with that bridge when I crossed it.

A few minutes later I sat with Stone in the basement and scanned through the file of information on the D&P Enterprise account, while Stone continued to sift through the trash. He hadn't uncovered anything else of interest in the bag of discarded paperwork. Stone obviously assumed Boris had shredded important documents and stuffed them in the trash bag. He was clearly disappointed.

Looking through the file I'd received from Mr. Myers, I discovered there were actually fourteen different accounts in D&P's name at the Rockdale Bank and Trust, but the sum total of all the balances was somewhat less than what I would've expected for a company with over sixty employees on their payroll. I recalled that Robert Fischer, the former loan officer at the bank, had remarked that a lot of their resources were in Swiss accounts. I continued to plow through the information.

I noticed each account at Rockdale Bank and Trust had a different name, such as "Mineral Rights" and "Precious Gems." It was clear D&P Enterprises had their fingers in many different pots. The account intriguing me the most was labeled "Miscellaneous." Among other things, it showed a monthly deposit of fifteen hundred dollars, drawn from the account of Harry Turner. Could this have something to do with the dirty laundry Alma Turner didn't want to have aired in public? I left Stone sorting through wads and slivers of paper, and went upstairs hoping to find the answer to that question.

I was walking down the hallway toward the parlor because I wanted to put the bank statement copies in my room. As I passed Boris Dack's suite across the hallway from mine, I heard the sound of a shower running. I knew I wasn't in my bathroom taking a shower, so I assumed it must be Boris taking one in his. Except for Rosalinda Swift and Cornelius Walker, Boris and I had the only bedroom suites on the first floor. The upper floor of the two-story home was made up of six guest rooms, all with private bathrooms attached. The top-story suites were slightly larger than the ones on the first floor, making them ideal for couples and distinguished guests. Stone used the owner's quarters, which included two sets of the upper-floor suites. The second set had been renovated into an office and large storage closet.

I tapped lightly on Boris's door. When he failed to answer, I gave it a nudge. The door was not locked and opened with a squeak into his room. I peeked inside and could see a light under the door of the closed bathroom. Steam escaped from the small gap above the door's threshold. Glancing around his room, I saw he'd laid a fresh suit on his bed, and atop his nightstand were his wallet, keys, pocket protector, and cell phone.

Quickly I picked up his cell phone, which was a Nokia model

similar to mine, and clicked on "calls" and then "outgoing" and found a number dialed at exactly six minutes after one that afternoon. I took a fancy ink pen from his pocket protector and copied the number onto the inside of my left wrist. While I was copying the last digits, I heard the shower stop. I tossed the pen on the nightstand, and quickly exited the room.

Halfway down the hallway, I realized I'd left the stack of bank statement copies on Boris's bed. I'd set them down to free up my hand to write the phone number on my wrist, and then forgot them in my haste to vacate the room. Now I had no choice but to risk being caught in Boris's bedroom because I had to retrieve the papers, if at all possible.

I rushed up the hall, nudged open his door again, relieved to discover the door to his restroom was still closed. What I'd have done had he been standing stark naked in the middle of his room, I'm not sure. Fortunately, for me, that wasn't the case.

I heard sounds coming from behind the still-closed bathroom door. It sounded as if Boris was hanging a towel on a towel rack and stepping into bathroom slippers. I grabbed the file off the bed and headed back out the door in one swift motion. As I stepped into the hallway, I caught a glimpse out of the corner of my eye of the bathroom door opening. I felt lightheaded after my frightfully close call as I unlocked the door to my room and quickly stepped inside.

I stashed the papers in the outer zippered pocket of my suitcase, and collapsed on my bed. My knees were shaking, and it took me several minutes to calm down. I went to the bathroom sink, splashed cold water on my face, and ran a brush through my hair. When I looked in the mirror I saw curly, highlighted hair that appeared dull and dry, and bloodshot, light-brown eyes with dark bags beginning to form beneath them. I was stunned by my own appearance. I needed a good night's sleep to recharge my internal battery.

Finally, I felt collected enough to make my way toward the parlor. I looked through the glass doors, as I passed the library, and noticed Alma Turner removing a book from the history section. Harry was not with her.

In the parlor, Rosalinda Swift was conversing with Cornelius Walker as they sat on high-backed chairs in front of a roaring fire in the fireplace. I heard Rosalinda titter after Cornelius said, "You see, I've always felt I was a lesbian trapped in a man's body."

I gave Cornelius's statement some consideration and then asked the pair if they'd seen Harry Turner recently. I soon realized Rosalinda wasn't tittering with amusement from Cornelius's quip, but rather, she was tanked out of her gourd. "Tarry Hurner?" she asked, as she tried to focus on me with her glazed and bloodshot eyes. "Tarry's not in dis woom white now, Wexie."

"Uh, yes, I can see Harry's not in the parlor, Rosalinda. Do you happen to know where exactly he is?"

Cornelius draped his arm around my shoulder, and pulled me toward him. "Rosalinda's had a long afternoon, my dear," he said. "Harry's out on the back porch, I believe. Would you like me to take you to him? Perhaps we can duck into the hall closet on the way. We should spend a few minutes getting better acquainted."

"No thanks, Cornelius. I can find him on my own. You stay here and keep an eye on Ms. Swift. She seems to be a bit under the weather."

"Don't worry, Lexie, she'll be all right. Doctor Walker will take care of Rosalinda."

I pulled away from Cornelius's embrace and excused myself. I was relieved Harry was, indeed, resting on the back deck, and he was alone. He was bundled up in a thick woolen scarf and a heavy parka, and was staring off into space, seemingly deep in thought. He stood next to the dirt-filled planter Otto had run his fingers through.

"Good afternoon, Mr. Turner," I said, in greeting. "Mind if I join you?"

"Not at all," he said, turning his attention toward me. "How are you feeling today, Lexie? You had us all worried last night. I can't imagine how you would come to swallow a poison like tansy oil. That's highly unusual."

"I know. I can't imagine it either, but I'm fine now. Thanks for asking. Do you mind if I ask you a personal question? It's something that's just come to my attention. It has me perplexed and more than a little curious."

"Depends on what you want to know, but I'll try to answer your question if I can."

"Harry, I can't explain how right now, but I've discovered you've been making a monthly stipend to D&P Enterprises. A check is written off your account on the first of each month in the amount of fifteen hundred dollars. The money doesn't appear to go toward a stock purchase or a deposit into a money market or mutual fund account. Were you a client of D&P Enterprises?"

"Um, well, no. Not exactly a client."

"Then why—"

"It's just, um, more of a matter of . . . well, let's put it this way. I'd be classified as more of a victim of D&P Enterprises than a client," Harry said softly. He cleared his throat and continued in a barely-audible whisper. "Listen, Lexie, can this be just between you and me? Alma would have a fit if she knew I told anyone about the blackmailing. For some reason, I feel like I can trust you."

"Blackmailing? Of course, Harry. I won't repeat what you say to anyone." Except for Stone, and possibly the entire team of homicide investigators, I thought, as I whispered back in response. "And I'm glad you feel you can trust me."

"Horatio has been blackmailing me for years, Lexie. He . . . he . . . uh—oh, this is so embarrassing. It was such a silly thing, really. Please keep this to yourself. Telling you about it is humiliating enough as it is."

"Go on, I won't spread it around. I promise you, Harry," I said, offering encouragement. Telling Stone, my boyfriend and co-conspirator, wasn't exactly spreading it around, was it? Oh yes, and possibly the team of homicide investigators, of course.

"All right, here goes," Harry said, lowering his head and refusing to look at me as he spoke. "About ten years ago, Horatio, who was an investor like myself, except on a grander scale, was attending the same antiques auction as I was. The auction was an estate sale in Jefferson City. We were both involved in a silent bid on a spectacular Salvador Dali original. I have a respectable art collection, although it's not nearly as impressive as Horatio's. Anyway, he'd booked a room at the hotel where I was staying. The night before the auction he burst into my room, uninvited, and caught me dressed up in a pair of pantyhose and one of Alma's frilly negligees. To this day, I don't know what possessed me to put those clothes on, but Horatio caught me completely off guard. Before I knew it, he had pulled one of those small, instamatic cameras from his pocket, snapped a photo of me, and departed. I merely tried the stuff on as a lark, you understand."

"Uh-huh, I see." I hoped I didn't look as astonished as I felt. Trying to visualize Harry Turner in panty hose and a frilly negligee was like trying to picture Mother Teresa in a thong bikini. Harry Turner was a very masculine-looking gentleman. Handsome and debonair, he had a Cary Grant aura. In many ways he'd initially reminded me of my own father, with his muscular build, dark hair and easygoing personality. He didn't remind me of my father anymore, however. My father would stick his arm down his own throat and rip out his heart before he'd don a woman's negligee and panty hose. There wasn't enough money stockpiled in all of Kansas City's casinos' vaults to entice him to sacrifice his manhood on a lark such as Mr. Turner just described. I knew I wasn't faring well in my attempt to mask my revulsion.

"Trust me, Lexie, it wasn't something I made a habit of doing. But I'd had a few drinks and was feeling kind of loopy and restless. Alma was at a ladies luncheon, and I'd picked her clothes up off the top of her suitcase to put them away. And, well, what can I say? I was bored, I guess. It was a bad decision, and I've regretted it every day of my life since. I certainly hope this doesn't color your view of me in any way."

That ship had sailed, I was afraid. I could never look at Harry in the same way again.

"I understand, Harry." Yeah, of course I understood. The guy was a closet transvestite. What's not to understand? I thought.

"So, I dropped out of the bidding, naturally, and left the auction," Harry continued. He wiped sweat off his forehead with a handkerchief he pulled from his back pocket. He looked like a man being ordered to walk down a gangplank. I knew this wasn't an easy story for him to relate.

"A few days later, a package arrived in my office with a copy of the photograph," Harry said. "There was no denying it was me in the photograph. Horatio had taken a full, clear shot of my face. I knew if the photo were ever made public, I'd be humiliated and my business would suffer irreparably. To keep it locked away in Horatio's safe would require a monthly payment of fifteen hundred dollars, he informed me in a note accompanying the photograph. I considered taking the package to the authorities but chickened out because I was too ashamed for them to see the photo. I knew most of the guys on the police force, and I didn't want to be the butt of a lot of jokes and ridicule. I was aware it was something apt to quickly spread all over town."

"Yes, I'm sure it would have, and I can see why you didn't want to bring it to the attention of the police. I wouldn't have, either, if I were in your shoes." Whether they were leather oxfords or sequined high heels, I said to myself.

"Not knowing what else to do, I reluctantly told Alma about it, and after a lot of deliberation, we agreed there was nothing we could do but pay the old bastard the money. Alma made it clear she'd divorce me should the photo ever see the light of day. That's what I meant when I said I would've done away with Horatio myself if I thought I could get away with it. He's made my life hell for the last decade. Alma and I are concerned about what will become of the contents of his safe, now that he's deceased. I'm sure Alma's threat to divorce me still stands. She's afraid of public humiliation and being ostracized by all the ladies at the country club.

"Alma and I have, understandably, grown apart in the intervening years, and it's not because I can't stand the thought of living without her. It's because she controls the purse strings in our family. If we were to divorce, I'd be left destitute, I'm sure."

Noticing the questioning look on my face, Harry added, "Our resources are primarily from an estate she inherited from a wealthy, unmarried aunt when Alma was only in her twenties. When we married, I was basically penniless. I had lots of grand ideas and high aspirations, but no money to back them. I don't need Alma in my life as much as I need her resources. I'm sure it sounds a bit mercenary to you, but I'm too old now to have to go out and pound the pavement looking for work to make a living. I'd rather leave matters as they are than to have to resort to being a vagrant."

"Yes, I can see why you'd be concerned about what might

happen with the contents of Mr. Prescott's safe," I said, not even bothering to temper my sarcasm. "But blackmail is illegal, and Horatio's actions were despicable. Does Boris know about the photo?"

"I'm not sure," Harry said. "But from the looks he sometimes gives me, and a few snide remarks he's made over the years, I'm relatively certain he does know about the photo. I've considered discussing the matter with him, but I'm not sure how to go about it. It's a difficult subject for me to broach, as I'm sure you can understand."

"Yes, I understand. It won't be easy, Harry, but I can't see you have much choice. If anyone would have access to Horatio's safe, it would be Boris. With Horatio's death, the circumstances surrounding the photo he took of you could be exposed to the general public. It may be something you'll want to ensure never happens. Have you ever had any personal differences with Boris?"

"No, I can't honestly say I've had any personal dealings with Boris at all. Dealing with Prescott was bad enough, and I've heard Boris is as greedy and unscrupulous as Horatio."

"Maybe it's time you found out for yourself what kind of guy Boris is. Stand up to him, try to cultivate a friendship with him, and then tell him the story in the same manner you just relayed it to me. Boris seems a bit gruff, but he may be more under-standing than you'd think. What have you got to lose at this point? You can't allow things to go on like this forever, can you?"

"No, I can't. You're right, Lexie. Maybe it's time I did just as you've suggested," Harry said. He ambled over and sat down on the veranda's swinging bench as if his knees would no longer support his body. After a long, awkward silence, Harry looked up at me and nodded. "I'm going to take your advice. Bless you, my girl. You've given me the confidence to do it. I'll speak with Boris about the situation and deal with the consequences. However it turns out, I know it will be easier than living with this hanging over my head another day. If Alma divorces me, I can always sue her for alimony—and move to another state where no one knows me."

I suddenly wished I had kept my mouth shut and prayed the suggestion I'd just made didn't blow up in Harry's face. The more I thought about it, the more I thought it was quite likely Boris had known about the blackmailing all along. He'd surely questioned Horatio about Harry Turner's payment being deposited in D&P's account on the first of every month. It wouldn't surprise me, now that Horatio was gone, if Boris didn't up the ante and demand a higher payment from Harry to continue to keep the photo a secret.

Oh, my, why did I always have to butt into other people's problems? When would I learn I couldn't shape the world and mould all of its inhabitants? I don't know why I felt it was my responsibility to persuade Harry to confront Boris about the blackmailing. I did know one thing, though. I would give just about anything I had to be a mouse in the corner of the room when this discussion between Harry and Boris transpired.

CHAPTER TEN

I was back in the basement with Stone following my conversation with Harry Turner. Stone had found little more of interest in the trash bag other than some vague information on bank accounts in Switzerland.

"Why are Swiss bank accounts so popular with money launderers?" I asked Stone because he seemed to know a little about everything.

"Due to Switzerland's neutrality, their banks tend to be the safest in the world," he said. "They allow depositors to be identified by a number known only to themselves and a minimum of bank officials. A private fortune can remain a secret because of this practice. If a bank employee violates this trust, he can be fined and imprisoned."

As Stone spoke, he continued to cram handfuls of shredded paper back into the trash bag, stopping for a few moments to inspect a small paper cut on his index finger. I watched him for a time, impressed once again with his vast knowledge. Then I remembered the phone number I'd jotted down on my wrist. Quickly I told Stone about my forage into Boris's room and about my close call in almost being caught going back for the bank statement papers. I dialed the number on my cell phone. While I listened to the phone ringing on the other end, I glanced at Stone. He didn't seem too pleased with me. He was shaking his head with a look of disapproval and running his fingers through his hair repeatedly.

The phone rang for a fourth time. I was disappointed when the call was answered by a voice mail recording. "Leave a message," was the extent of the coarse message. I'd hoped for something a little more informative, like, "You've reached Joe Blow, President of Embezzlers Anonymous. I'm currently away from the phone, doing time in Leavenworth on an extortion charge. You may contact my attorney at 1-800-GO2-JAIL or press one to record a voice mail after the beep." But, unfortunately, "Leave a message," was all I got.

"Damn!" I said out loud.

"No luck, huh?"

"No." An earlier thought about being a mouse in the room when Harry confronted Boris crossed my mind. Maybe I couldn't actually be a mouse, but I might be able to hide like one. "Say, Stone, do you think there's enough room under the bed in Boris's room for me to hide while he takes that six o'clock phone call tonight?"

Stone shook his head in dismay. "Yes, there's enough room, and no, you aren't going to try something risky like that. Sneaking into Boris's room while he showered was risky enough and not very sensible on your part. The success of this inn is nowhere near so important to me that I'm going to let you put yourself in any more dangerous positions like the one you put yourself in today. So erase the idea from your mind and forget about it, Lexie. I mean it. It's much too dangerous. Men like Boris Dack can be ruthless and unpredictable."

I nodded, but in the back of my mind I still tossed the idea around. I couldn't help it. I was bristling with curiosity about the phone call Boris was expecting. An impulsive nature like mine was very hard to keep in check. I'd had to deal with the consequences of that fact my entire life.

Crystal had the master key to his room. I could come up with some excuse to borrow it while she was busy frying chicken for supper. Supper was at 6:30. I'd surely be back in the kitchen by then. I assumed Boris would return to the parlor after taking his phone call and partake in the social drinking before the guests gathered in the dining room for supper. If I remembered right, the bed in his room was like mine. It was a large, four-poster bed, set high off the floor, with a dust ruffle hanging quite low. I didn't think Boris could bend over far enough to peer under the bed, even if he wanted to.

And didn't I owe it to Stone to help him in any way I could? He'd certainly sacrificed a lot to help me when Wendy had been abducted in New York the previous fall. I managed to convince myself that when it was all over and nothing bad had happened to me, he'd see the whole thing differently.

I was still feeling a bit weak from the tansy oil poisoning, so I took a short nap in the afternoon. Following a series of nightmarish dreams, I woke up drenched in sweat. None of the dreams made any sense at all, but they were enough to scare me in to a wide-awake state. In one dream Cornelius, who was dressed only in a g-string and cowboy boots, was chasing me down an alley.

I shook my head to clear it and took several deep breaths. I then quickly showered, changed, and went downstairs to help Crystal prepare the evening meal. If nothing else, the power nap had boosted my energy level.

Happy hour wouldn't begin for another hour, but Rosalinda, Cornelius, and the Poffenbargers were already having drinks in the parlor. This wasn't unexpected, for there was little else to do at the inn except indulge in social drinking and visit with other guests. Our guests seemed to be well schooled on drinking and idle chatter.

"Getting a head start on happy hour?" I asked the group in a cheerful voice.

"For now we're just having some lemonade to wash down a few crackers," Patty said. Otto nodded, as he executed an open-aired quasi-toast in my direction. Cornelius followed suit, and Rosalinda nodded also but kept her glass tightly clutched between her hands. She was taking no chances on letting her drink make an escape.

"Otto, as a botanist, you might be just the person I need to answer a question for me," I said. I sat down on the armrest of the sofa as I spoke.

"I'll do my best, Lexie," Otto said.

"As I'm sure you've heard, I somehow ingested a toxic substance called tansy oil last evening. Oddly enough, the same substance was found in Horatio Prescott's system during his autopsy."

"You don't say! I'd heard about your experience, but I didn't know Horatio had been poisoned, too. How extremely odd!"

"Yes, I thought so, too. What can you tell me about tansy oil? I've never heard of it before." Otto knew all about the toxic quality of the autumn crocus, so I hoped he was well versed in tansy oil, as well. I wasn't disappointed.

"Tansy is an herb which was once regarded by gypsies as a cure-all for numerous medical conditions like expelling tape worms, preventing miscarriages, and easing dyspepsia."

"Dyspep—?"

"Indigestion. But tansy oil can be highly lethal. As little as one or two tablespoons can cause death. Tansy oil is high in thujone, a poison that causes convulsions, seizures, vomiting, organ degeneration, or even respiratory arrest." Otto spoke in a monotone, as if reciting information from a textbook. "Tansy is also known as bachelors' button and scented fern."

"Are you kidding? I have bachelor button plants in my flower garden. Where would one purchase tansy oil around here? I assume the extraction of the oil is a complicated procedure an average layperson like myself wouldn't even try to attempt."

"The oil is extracted by steam distillation. I imagine most people would obtain it through a specialty store." Otto said this in a tone indicating he obtained his own toxic oils by steam distillation, and looked down upon anyone who had to stoop to buying their tansy oil at a store. He went on to say, "I'm sure the Rockdale Farm and Ranch Supply store has a limited herb section, so it's possible they might carry it, but I doubt it. You might ask Cornelius, though. He's one of the managers of the store and has worked for them for years, since they first opened their doors."

Hmm. So Cornelius might have easy access to tansy oil? Could the Don Juan of manure be acting out of retribution for the loss of his beloved Ethel? I put "visit Farm and Ranch store" on my mental list of things to accomplish tomorrow.

"The Latin name for tansy is 'tanacetum.' " Otto continued, but I had tuned him out. My mind was racing ahead to other matters I needed to attend to.

Patty swallowed the last of the cheese crackers on the snack tray and yawned. "Shut up already! Ms. Starr doesn't care what the Latin name is, nor does anyone else in the room. You can be so utterly boring, Otto. Sometimes, I don't know why I put up with you. No one is impressed with your ability to recite tedious details."

I hated myself momentarily for agreeing with Patty. I felt bad I had caused Otto to be subjected to Patty's sharp tongue, but Otto seemed unaffected. He was accustomed to insults and the brash treatment he received at regular intervals from his wife.

I smiled at Otto and said, "Thanks for the info, Mr. Poffenbarger. I was fairly confident you'd be able to answer my question. Relax and enjoy your lemonade, everyone. I need to help Crystal with supper. Hope you all like southern fried chicken, mashed potatoes, gravy, and zucchini squash."

"I, for one, am not at all hungry," Patty said. "The stress of this whole ordeal has put me 'off my feed,' as they say. But despite my lack of appetite, I guess I'll have to try to eat a few bites. For the sake of my health, you understand."

"Of course. I understand. I'm sure you'll manage to get something down, Mrs. Poffenbarger," I said, exiting the room.

Crystal was in the kitchen paring potatoes. She looked fresh and energetic. I felt like a slug with salt raining down on me in comparison. I needed something other than coffee to perk me up, something cold and refreshing. Lemonade sounded good to me.

"Do we have any more lemonade, Crystal?"

"No, except for a few cans still in the freezer. I just served the last of it to Mr. Walker and the Poffenbargers."

"And Rosalinda? Isn't she drinking lemonade, too?" I asked, reaching into the refrigerator for a can of Diet Coke in lieu of lemonade.

Crystal chuckled and said, "Not hardly. But I'm sure there's so much vodka and so little orange juice in her screwdriver that it looks like lemonade. Rosalinda's happy hour started just after lunch, Lexie. I can't believe she's still conscious."

"She was clinging to her glass as if it were the only thing keeping her upright."

"I can well imagine. How are you doing, by the way?"

"I'm much better. I'm sorry I wasn't around to help you this morning," I said.

"No problem. And it's not like you could help it. I'm just sorry to hear about what happened to you last night. I couldn't believe it when Stone told me all about it early this morning right after I arrived," she said, placing the pan of potatoes on the stove and the paring knife in the dishwasher as she spoke. "I'm lucky Stone was up and about early today. I forgot my key at home. I sat it down on our kitchen table at home while I opened the back door to let the dogs inside, and then I forgot and left without it."

"Maybe we should consider hiding a spare key under a flower pot or something. Any one of us could accidentally lock ourselves out," I said.

"Yeah, maybe we should," Crystal said. She moved around the room like a ballerina while I staggered around it like a wild boar on tranquilizers. Crystal glanced at me, concern showing on her face, although she made no comment about my sluggishness. I was still feeling the effects of the tansy oil I'd ingested the night before.

"Why would anyone poison you?" Crystal asked. "Who would want to do something like that?"

"I wish I knew," I said sincerely. I sat down heavily on the chair Crystal offered.

"By the way, Lexie, I found something that might be of interest to you while I was cleaning the guest rooms this morning."

"What's that?"

"I found this," she said, pulling a thick manuscript from a kitchen cabinet. She placed it on the counter beside me.

"Is this Mr. Prescott's book?" I asked, in a soft whisper.

"Yes, but it wasn't in Mr. Prescott's room," Crystal whispered back. "It was in the Poffenbargers' room, inside Otto Poffenbarger's suitcase. I found it when I picked up the suitcase to vacuum under it. The weight of the manuscript caused the suitcase to plop open, and the papers scattered all over the floor. I put them all back in order and brought the manuscript down here to hide in the cabinet. I didn't want Mr. Poffenbarger to know I was the one who confiscated it. I'm still worried about what will happen if he finds out. Whoever's responsible for all that's happened is obviously capable of doing anything to anyone who gets in his way."

"That's true," I said. "But it's interesting that Otto would have Horatio's manuscript in his baggage. Otto's writing a book similar to the one Horatio was writing."

"I know. That's what Stone told me this morning. Which is why I thought it was odd to find the manuscript in Mr. Poffen-barger's suitcase."

"I think it's odd, too. You don't suppose—?"

"I don't know," Crystal said, still whispering.

"Why don't you put this back up into the cabinet for now, okay?" I said. "I'm going to talk to Stone and see if he thinks we should alert the authorities. I'll be back shortly to lend a hand in the kitchen. And don't worry about Mr. Poffenbarger finding out. We won't tell him it was you who found the manuscript in his bag and turned it over to us."

"Thanks, and take your time. I shouldn't need much help with supper, Lexie. I'm ahead of schedule as it is. I'd rather you took it easy tonight. Put your feet up and rest a while after you speak with Stone. You had a nasty experience yesterday, and you don't want to overdo it and bring on a relapse."

I knew she'd been speaking with Stone. He'd made the same comment, verbatim, just minutes earlier. I thanked her, left the kitchen, and detoured back through the parlor to find Stone. By now, Rosalinda was asleep, or passed out, in the over-stuffed chair facing the fireplace, and Cornelius was lounging in the chair across from her. The Poffenbargers were just rising from the matching couch. Patty let out a loud grunt as she hoisted herself off the cushion. "We're going to go back to our room to shower and freshen up. Maybe I can work up an appetite before supper," she said. I forced a smile in response to her comment and turned toward her slim husband.

"Otto, remember telling me yesterday that Mr. Prescott was writing a book about the proper way to go about restoring historic homes, a book similar to the one you're working on?"

"Yes, of course, I remember."

"The investigators indicated they'd like to look at the manuscript for potential clues, but they haven't been able to locate it. Have you any ideas where he usually keeps it?"

"I've never known him to leave home without it," Otto said. "I'll bet money he brought it with him to the inn to work on in his spare time. I know he was being pressured by the publishing house to complete it. The investigators must have overlooked it. It's surely in his room or, at the very least, somewhere here at the inn. I'd suggest they search this entire place again."

Otto sounded so sincere, I found it difficult to believe he could have snatched the manuscript from Horatio's room. Would he have said Horatio wouldn't have arrived without it if he didn't want anyone to know it was missing? Would he suggest the investigators should search the entire inn again if the manuscript was in his possession, in his unzipped luggage where it could be easily detected? It didn't make any sense to me at all. But could I trust Otto Poffenbarger? Could I trust any of the Historical Society guests? There was at least one person here I couldn't trust; that much was obvious. As Crystal had said, that particular person was capable of doing anything to anyone who got in his way. And somehow I had to determine who the person was before he made another attempt at killing me—and possibly succeeded.

CHAPTER ELEVEN

I found Stone on the back deck visiting with Boris Dack, who was nervously puffing on a pencil-thin, horrid-smelling cigar. Boris checked the time on his watch at least seven times during the five minutes I was outside on the deck. Stone winked at me when Boris glanced away for a few seconds. We both knew Boris was anxious not to miss his six o'clock phone call, but only I knew I was planning on not missing it either.

"Good evening, Mr. Dack," I said. Once again I used the weather to make idle chatter. "I see it's beginning to snow again. Big flakes too, aren't they?"

"Yeah, big flakes."

"That's sure an unusual scent for a cigar, but I like it. What kind is it?"

"Cuban." Boris was clearly not interested in discussing snowflakes or cigars with someone he considered nothing more than a chambermaid. He had more important things on his mind than the scent of his tobacco—like positive news from Shorty about some "damn birds."

"Oh, I see. Yes, I guess I've always heard Cuban cigars were the best. By the way, do you know if Horatio Prescott smoked? There were ashes found in his ashtray, which the investigators seem to think is a little strange," I said. Or, at least, I was certain they would have thought it a little strange had they noticed the ashes and known Horatio was a non-smoker. Boris gave me a curious look and shrugged nonchalantly.

"The ashes were probably mine," he said, after a long silence. He continued in his usual annoying way, spouting ten-letter words at will. "I'd stopped by his room to expostulate his proposal for a highly speculative investment. It was an ephemeral visit, you understand, but it stands to reason I was smoking at the time. I usually enjoy several cigars after supper."

"What was Horatio's physical condition at the time, that evening when you spoke to him in his room?" Stone asked. "Do you recall?"

"He did seem a bit inarticulate and disjointed at the time, now that I think about it. In retrospect, I suppose I should've questioned him about his condition since he was kind of wobbly. I just assumed he'd had one too many scotch and waters after supper, which was standard operating procedure for him. He cast aspersions on me about smoking all the time, but he habitually drank a lot more than I ever did. Thinking back, I'm convinced it may have been the poison making him acting so anomalously."

"Anomalously?" I asked.

"Queerly, abnormally, strangely, oddly" he said, in simpler terms.

Was the grapevine in full operation? Were all the guests now aware of the attempted poisoning of Prescott? Could the word have spread that rapidly since I mentioned the matter in the parlor? I wondered how Boris knew about it. Perhaps Stone had told him. He'd spoken with Boris on several occasions, both this morning and this evening.

"In what way was Mr. Prescott behaving queerly last night?" I asked Boris.

"Oh, he seemed kind of ill, light-headed and dizzy. His speech was nearly incoherent. It was out of character for him to show any kind of weakness at all. He normally handled his liquor better than that. He was reacting much like I was told you reacted to the tansy oil someone slipped you."

"So you heard about the tansy oil incident, huh? It's nasty stuff, let me tell you."

"Yes, and I'm sorry to hear you also had an encounter with it." Boris didn't sound sincerely sorry, but I had to give him credit for trying.

Boris and I checked our watches simultaneously. I realized I'd have to get the master key from Crystal and up to Boris's room soon if I were going to try to eavesdrop on his important phone call. I'd tell Stone about the manuscript later. Excusing myself, I returned to the kitchen.

Crystal was standing at the stove arranging wings, thighs, and breasts in a skillet of sizzling grease. I noticed her ring of room keys lying on the counter next to her purse. I picked them up and crossed to the door. "Stone needs to borrow your keys for just a few minutes, Crystal," I said. "He can't seem to find his at the moment. It seems as if keeping track of keys is a recurring problem today."

I rushed away without giving Crystal an opportunity to respond to my confiscation of her keys, as if her approval was without doubt. I glanced out on the deck to make sure Boris hadn't already left. He was snubbing his cigar in an ashtray, so I knew he'd be going to his room soon.

Praying that opting to eavesdrop wasn't a decision I'd live to regret, I raced down the hall and used the key marked "#3" to unlock the door to Boris's room. As quickly as I could, I slid under his bed, positioning myself as far to the back as possible, on the opposite side of the nightstand that held some personal items he'd unloaded from his pockets. He was a flabby, heavy-set man, and I didn't want to be flattened under the springs if he sat down on the bed.

I scarcely had time to find a comfortable position when I heard Boris enter the room and unclip the cell phone from his belt. He placed it on the bed. He muttered under his breath. All I could make out were two words: "bitch" and "nosy"—and not necessarily in that order. Aha. It seemed his opinion of me was no more flattering than my opinion of him.

I could hear the ticking of his alarm clock as I tried to remain still under the bed. It reminded me of the one time I'd had a CT-scan at the hospital. I suddenly itched in places I didn't know a person could itch, and I felt as if I were afflicted with restless leg syndrome. Even my eyelashes developed instant nervous tics. Soon I felt myself gasping, as if all the oxygen under the bed had been depleted. I was sure Boris could hear my labored breathing. I thought I might be experiencing an ill-timed panic attack. The next five minutes dragged on for at least two and a half hours, or so it seemed.

Finally, Boris's cell phone rang with the sound of a 1940's show tune that seemed totally inappropriate for the circumstances. I had to bite my lip to suppress a giggle. At least the bout of anxiety had eased, and I was breathing normally again, for a short while at least.

"Yeah?" Boris said in a gruff, impatient tone. I could only hear his side of the conversation, but I had a pretty good idea of what was going on.

"Tomorrow? You positive, Shorty?" he asked. I listened to his responses as he conversed with a man called Shorty. I tried to picture Shorty, whom I figured was either four foot ten, or seven feet tall. It wasn't a nickname you gave to a man with average height, in the same way you didn't call an average-sized guy, "Slim."

"How many kakapos did you get?" I heard Boris ask. "Two pair? Good, that's damned good, kid! Any problem getting on or off the island? Good. Uh-huh, yeah I understand. Uh-huh. Where are they holding them now? Yeah, I see. I expect you to make an expeditious trip to get them back here."

He paused a moment to listen to the caller's response, and then said, "It means 'fast,' Shorty. Make it a fast trip. Okay? But take good care of them, you hear? One of them croaks, and I'll shove the dead parrot up your skinny ass. You understand me, kid?"

Dead parrot? Kakapos? I needed to go straight to Stone's room to use his computer as soon as I left Boris's room. I tried to picture my aunt's cockapoo, Max, with a parrot on his head, to use as word association, so I wouldn't forget the word he'd used: kakapo. Max was a cocker spaniel/poodle mix, and, strangely, I found it less confusing than picturing a cockatoo, which really was a parrot, with a crested thing on top of its head. But Boris had definitely said kakapo, not cockatoo. Oh, wow. I needed air. I felt as if I were beginning to hyperventilate.

I tried to take my mind off breathing, hoping I would resume normal breathing again if I didn't work so hard at it. Instead, I concentrated on Boris's voice as he spoke again. "I want to make the exchange tomorrow night. Pablo Pikstone won't wait forever, you know. I'm holding you to your promise, Shorty. Got it? Screw me over and when you wake up again, you'll think a loaded garbage truck has run you down. Yeah, yeah, okay. No, I'm not worried about him finding out. I told you, he's dead now, Shorty. No, I don't know who popped the old bastard, but I'm happy as hell somebody did. He was getting to be a royal pain in my ass. Trying to catch me in the act of screwing him over, while the whole time he was screwing me over every chance he got."

So, according to Boris anyway, he didn't know who killed Horatio, but he was pleased about his death. I'd figured as much. And basically, it turned out, Boris and Horatio were two crooks, trying to out-crook each other.

I was trying to use word association again to remember the name Pablo Pikstone and tried visualizing Pablo Picasso perched on a large rock, painting a picture of my Water-Pik, when I realized that Boris had ended the call. As I heard him fold his cell phone in half, the room phone on his nightstand rang.

"Yeah?" I heard him say again. "No thanks, Stone. I had a late lunch, and way too many stuffed mushrooms and hot wings during happy hour. I think I'll skip supper and get a good night's rest tonight. I'll see you in the morning before I check out."

Uh-oh. I didn't like his comments at all. I looked out from under the dust ruffle just in time to see a pair of wadded up socks hit the floor. One sock was black and one was dark blue, so I gathered Boris might be afflicted with color-blindness. I'd read most people with the condition were male.

Next came the sound of a brass belt buckle landing on the throw rug with a dull, muffled thud. Then I heard the faint whir of a zipper being unfastened as Boris let loose a crude belch at the same time. I felt a sick queasiness in my stomach.

Just as I began to fear I was in for a very long night, I felt the beginning of a sneeze. I fought it as best I could, but it was a losing battle. I managed to stifle the sneeze to a dainty little "choo," which Boris would have definitely heard, anyway, had it not been synchronized perfectly with a loud rap on the door.

"Boris? Mr. Dack?" I heard Stone's voice outside the door. He sounded anxious, but his voice was the most welcome sound I'd heard in ages. When Boris opened his door, Stone said, "You have an incoming call on the kitchen phone. Crystal took the call but couldn't give the caller the private number to the phone in this room because she didn't know it."

"Okay. Give me a moment then," Boris said with irritation obvious in his voice.

"Uh, Mr. Dack, you don't need to put your shoes on to go to the kitchen, but you probably should zip your zipper. Crystal said the guy sounded really impatient."

A few seconds later, Stone was peering under the bed, grabbing me by the ankle and sliding me out across the shiny wood floor. I felt like a human dust mop. I could tell by the angry look of frustration in his eyes that he was very upset with me.

"We'll talk later," he said sternly, and hurried me out of Boris's room and pushed me into mine across the hall. He closed my door soundlessly, leaving me inside. I was trembling, more in anticipation of Stone's response to my eavesdropping than in reaction to my close call in Boris's room.

A few seconds later, I heard Stone say, "Really? The caller must have been extremely impatient. Well, I'm sorry, Mr. Dack, but I'm sure he'll call back. I'll give Crystal the number for the phone in your room when I inform her that you won't be joining us for supper. Good night, Mr. Dack. I'll see you in the morning."

A few seconds later the door to my room was flung open, and Stone stepped inside. He whispered in a forceful manner. "What in the name of hell were you thinking, Lexie? As soon as Crystal mentioned you'd borrowed her set of keys, I knew exactly what you'd done. I just knew. And frankly, it scared me half to death. There's no telling what a man like Boris Dack is capable of when he's backed into a corner. I thought I'd made it clear I didn't want you to attempt anything so risky."

"And I thought I'd made it clear I'm an adult and can make my own decisions," I said, knowing it was a stupid and immature thing to say. Stone was only concerned about my well-being. He wasn't trying to force his will on me for his own amusement. I knew I was still trying to adjust to the novelty of having a man around to look out for me and protect me from the consequences of my impulsive actions. I'd been on my own for nearly twenty years, and I was very set in my ways. I was born under the sign of Aries, after all, and impulsiveness was a curse I was born with, according to all the astrologers. And saddled with forever, I had no doubt. Acting spontaneously was not something I could just give up the way I'd given up cigarettes.

"I know you're an adult. I just wish you would behave like one!"

I opened my mouth to make a crude retort and then closed it immediately. This was the first time the two of us had ever exchanged cross words. It occurred to me then that Stone wasn't upset because I'd behaved childishly or against his wishes. He was upset because I had placed myself in a precarious position, a situation that could have come to a lot more ghastly conclusion than it did. What would I have done if Boris Dack had heard me sneezing under his bed and Stone had not been there to rescue me? What would Boris have done?

"You're right, Stone—"

"Lexie, I'm sorry—"

"No, you're right. Eavesdropping on Boris Dack's conversation was a stupid thing to do, and I apologize. I just couldn't stand not knowing what the six o'clock phone call was all about. I'm still not sure, but I know more than I did before. Please don't be mad at me."

"I'm not mad at you, and I'm sorry I yelled at you," he said as he put his arms around me and pulled me into an embrace. "I love you, Lexie, and the thought of anything happening to you . . . well, I didn't handle the situation very well, I guess."

"I love you, too, Stone. Thanks for rescuing me just in the nick of time. Remind me to have Crystal run a mop under all the beds tomorrow. The dust bunnies were launching me into a sneezing fit. And Stone, you handled this incident tonight like a pro. I'll try to be more careful in the future and not put you in the position of having to handle my problems so frequently. My actions tonight were thoughtless and reckless, and I'll try my best to see such a thing doesn't happen again, or at least not very often."

I stopped short of making any rash promises because I knew myself well enough to know my impulsiveness was sometimes impossible to keep in check.

"Thank you. I'd appreciate if you were more cautious, more often. That's all I can ask for, I guess. More often."

We shared a long kiss and an even longer hug, and then I reiterated what I'd heard Boris say on the phone. Stone had never heard of a "kakapo" either, and agreed I should perform a Google search on his computer. He handed me the keys to his room and office, which I shoved into my pocket.

"Would you stay with me in my room tonight, Lexie?"

"I thought we'd agreed if we had guests in the inn, we shouldn't—"

"That was before all this happened. Now, with the current circumstances being what they are, I'd feel better having you where I can keep an eye on you. Besides, I've missed you." Stone reached around to cup the cheeks of my posterior in his hands and pull me toward him. He'd made his message quite clear. He squeezed my butt cheeks tenderly, and said, "I sleep better when I have you next to me."

"I've missed you, too. And I'd definitely feel safer and sleep more soundly with you beside me. The fingernail file I keep under my pillow offers a very limited sense of security."

"Okay. Then it's settled. By the way, you do know who Pablo Pikstone is, don't you?" Stone asked me.

"No, I don't think I've ever heard of him."

"He's the eccentric billionaire who lives just outside Blue Springs. He has a large estate off I-70, and he houses lions, tigers, monkeys, alligators, and all kinds of other wild and exotic animals on his property. A ten-foot tall fence surrounds the entire compound with razor-sharp barbs across the top. It looks like a prison yard. He has several zoo-keepers and animal trainers on his payroll."

"Oh, yes, I do remember the place now. Wasn't there a lot of controversy with the animal rights activists a few years ago? About him illegally keeping endangered species or something like that?"

"I wouldn't doubt it. He probably gave a huge cash donation to all their assorted non-profit animal rights organizations just to get them off his back. He certainly wouldn't contribute for the sake of the animals. But money can be a powerful incentive, you know. It's unfortunate, though, because something needs to be done to protect those animals. They shouldn't be forced to live in cages the way they frequently are. I can't even stand to visit a zoo for that very reason."

I agreed, and then excused myself to go to the kitchen to help Crystal finish the supper preparations. I felt guilty for having heaped so much responsibility on our already overworked young helper.

Crystal did not look overworked when I arrived in the kitchen. She was smiling and humming as she dished up the mashed potatoes with a large silver spoon. I noticed she'd already set the table. She waved off my apology and motioned for me to move the zucchini from the stove to the serving dish. I told her Boris would be skipping supper, and I removed one of the place settings when I took the zucchini and potatoes into the dining room. A large platter of fried chicken was already in the middle of the large table with smaller bowls of gravy, olives, sliced tomatoes, and celery sticks, arranged around it. The scene was so appealing and the aroma so enticing, it made my mouth water.

Crystal followed me in the room with a basket of hot, steaming dinner rolls and a tub of whipped butter. I looked up at the clock on top of the china hutch as it chirped half past the hour.

The guests began to enter the dining room to take their places at the table. Patty led the pack, as usual. I hoped she'd be able to force a little food down her gullet, even though she'd been off her feed recently. By the gleam in her eyes, and the licking of her lips, I didn't think this was going to be a major problem.

CHAPTER TWELVE

"Agh! Eech! Bleeck!"

Everyone at the table stopped chewing to look in horror at Patty Poffenbarger, who was choking on something she'd just attempted to swallow. Soon the sounds of agony ceased when she could no longer draw any air down her windpipe. Her face began to turn a vivid color of purple as she grasped her throat in terror. Her multiple chins were quivering like a mouse in a snake's cage. It wasn't a pretty sight.

Otto sat beside his wife as motionless as a Vatican guard, in a state of helpless panic. The only one who didn't seem to be frozen in time was Stone, who jumped to his feet and darted around the table in a flash. He wrapped his arms around Patty's ample abdomen, his hands clenched together under her sternum. He then executed the Heimlich maneuver in one deft upward and inward thrust.

Nothing happened. Patty continued to flail her arms and turn deeper shades of purple. Stone tried again, and again, nothing happened.

Finally, on his fourth attempt, there was a distinct *whoosh* as a small piece of chicken bone flew across the table and landed with a muted splash in the gravy boat. Eleven pairs of eyes stared at the bone floating on top of the chicken gravy as if waiting for it to perform a soft shoe act for their entertainment. Almost in unison, everybody at the table placed their silverware across their plates and scooted their chairs back away from the table. Supper was officially over. I'd already put my silverware down and was thinking back to the comment I'd made to Wendy about chicken bones being hazardous to one's health. Had I somehow had a premonition of this near-tragedy? Or had I jinxed Patty Poffenbarger into nearly choking to death?

"Why, I never!" Patty exclaimed once she could speak again. "I ought to sue this abhorrent establishment for every dime I can squeeze out of it! Serving chicken with the bones still intact? What in God's name were you thinking? Good grief. I could have died right here at this very table! Don't think for one damned second you're going to get away with this kind of—of—uh, negligence!"

Otto Poffenbarger stared at his wife as if he were just seeing her for the first time. A look of pure disgust came over his face, and he spoke out with an assertiveness even he couldn't have known he possessed. "Shut up, you fool. You owe your life to Mr. Van Patten, Patricia. It was he, the owner of this *abhorrent* establishment, who kept you from keeling over dead from nothing more than your own obsessive gluttony. It certainly wasn't his fault you were stuffing yourself like a Christmas turkey. If not for him, you very well would have died at this table, and you owe him your utmost gratitude for reacting as he did and saving your fat ass!"

For the next few seconds, you could have heard a fly pass gas in the dining room. Otto was livid, pointing his finger in fury at his spouse, who was beginning to turn purple again—but this time from mortification. It was safe to assume she'd never seen Otto take a stance like this before. He normally let her play him like a four-stringed banjo. But not today.

"There shouldn't have been any bones in the—"

"Shut up, I said!" Otto commanded. "I've heard enough out of you for one night. Everyone at this table has heard enough out of you! Chickens have bones, you dolt. They always have had bones, and they always will have bones. You should be smart enough to know you can't gulp fried chicken down like a bowl of tomato soup. It's not like you haven't been shoving it in your face for years. And nobody claimed we were having de-boned chicken for supper, did they? Well? Did they?"

Patty began to respond but thought better of it. She clamped her lips together and struggled to her feet. Otto used his left hand to grasp her elbow to lead her away from the table and his right to shake hands with Stone. "We owe you our deepest appreciation for your quick thinking and action. There'll be no more mention of lawsuits—of any kind. I promise. You've been a most gracious host, and we're in your debt, Stone. Thank you."

Stone patted Otto's shoulder, and replied, "You're welcome, sir."

Otto waved at Crystal as he turned to escort his seething spouse from the room. "And thank you, young lady, for another delicious supper."

"Boorish hog," I heard Crystal mutter under her voice as she left the dining room. I had to agree with Crystal and was amused at her assessment of Mrs. Poffenbarger. She wasn't aware I'd heard her comment, so I didn't embarrass her by mentioning it.

After I'd carried all the dirty supper dishes to the kitchen, Crystal dealt with the leftovers, and I began loading the dishwasher. In unspoken agreement, all of the leftover chicken was hurled into the trashcan so as not to be a gruesome reminder the next day of the choking incident.

As I added Cascade to the dishwasher's reservoirs, I noticed Crystal's normal rosy complexion had suddenly taken on an ashen appearance. It was apparent she was thinking about the near-tragedy and beginning to feel personally responsible for the bone that had lodged in Patty's throat. "Lexie, maybe I should have—"

"It's not your fault, Crystal. There's absolutely no way you could have prevented what happened. De-boning chicken before you fry it is not common practice. Like Otto said, the woman was gorging herself with no thought of being cautious of the bones that are always found in southern fried chicken," I said. "You've had a very long day, my dear. Why don't you call it a night and let me finish up in here? You've got to be back here early in the morning. And beyond everything else, it's snowing outside. You'll want to get home before it gets too slick or deep."

"Yes, you're probably right," Crystal said, looking out the window at the snow melting as it landed on the sidewalk. For the first time since I'd met the young woman, she appeared weary and distracted. Gone was her normal gregarious personality.

"If you have any trouble getting out in the morning, call me here and I'll come pick you up in my Jeep. It's got four-wheel-drive, of course."

"I live in St. Joseph, you know, not Rockdale," Crystal said.

"That's okay. I can find it if you give me directions. I don't mind driving the extra distance at all."

"All right, I'll head home. And I promise to call in the morning if I can't get my car out. It doesn't do real well on snow or slick roads, and sometimes the old clunker won't even start in cold weather."

Crystal bundled up in her coat and knit hat in preparation to leave. "Good night. See you tomorrow."

"Good night, dear. Thanks for all your hard work today."

After the kitchen was gleaming again, I made a fresh pot of de-caf, poured myself a cup, and put the rest into a pump-style thermos. I sat it out on a cart in the parlor in case any of the guests decided to look for a cup of after-supper coffee. I added a few small saucers, forks, napkins, and an apple-strudel crumb cake Crystal had baked earlier in the day. I was sure Patty Poffenbarger, given a little time to recover from her near-death experience, would be back in the kitchen before retiring, attempting to stave off starvation. After all, supper had been cut short, and she needed to eat to keep up her strength. She did have a pesky thyroid condition to cope with.

CHAPTER THIRTEEN

I took my coffee and retreated to Stone's office. I booted up his computer and logged on to the Internet. First I did a cross-check on the phone number I'd transferred from my wrist to my notebook before scrubbing it off with a bar of Lava soap. The number belonged to someone named Mortimer Sharp, according to the online phone directory. I jotted the name down in the notebook.

Next, I typed "kakapo" into the keyword box and clicked on the "search" button. Before long I knew more about the critically endangered parrot species called the kakapo than I'd ever expected to know. Kakapo meant "night parrot" in the Maori language, and the remaining eighty-six kakapos in existence were located on the offshore islands of New Zealand. So what could this possibly have to do with Boris? I wondered.

The kakapo was the only nocturnal parrot, as well as the largest, the longest living, and the only flightless parrot. Strict vegetarians, they hopped like sparrows, and they growled like dogs. They had strong, fruity scents, making them easy to detect by their predators: cats, rats, ferrets, possums and stoats. This had been a contributing factor to their decrease in numbers, I read on the computer screen.

I clicked on a link that took me to the home page of the New Zealand Department of Conservation where I found a lot of information about the current program to protect and increase the kakapo population. Each parrot was fitted with a radio transmitter and a microchip for individual identification. They were constantly monitored by a staff of six people, all of whom were dedicated to the preservation of the dwindling parrot species. They'd actually managed to increase the kakapo population to eighty-six from sixty-four the previous year, so the program was having some measured success in its endeavors to bring the bird back from the brink of extinction. Now I was even less convinced Boris was involved with one or more of the eighty-six kakapos in existence. But I continued to read on.

The staff members gave the kakapos regular health checks, supplemental feedings, and were involved in predator control and artificial incubation, and also in the hand-raising of the newly hatched chicks. Although it sounded like a somewhat enviable job, the DOC staff worked long, hard hours in less than ideal conditions.

I clicked on another link to take me to a page of recent media releases. I noticed one release had just been posted earlier in the day. *Four Kakapos Abducted from Transfer Pen* was the headline.

According to the article, two pair of adult kakapos had been snatched in the dead of night from a holding pen where they were awaiting a transfer back to Whenua Hou, or Codfish Island, scheduled to occur in three days time.

Basil, Gunner, Bella, and Maggie were all part of the complicated breeding program and had been undergoing examinations to ascertain that they were fit for mating. The kakapos' main source of food was the rimu and kahikatea fruits, and during years such as this, when the fruits were plentiful, mating and breeding was most successful.

When the designated staff members made their early morning rounds to check on the welfare of the foursome, they were devastated to discover the four birds had been covertly removed overnight from their holding pens.

Although Te Kakahu, or Chalky Island, where the parrots

were being held in a transfer pen, was only accessible by plane or helicopter and unauthorized landings were prohibited, there was evidence that a small chopper had landed in a remote site on the island during the night. Wire cutters and other tools had been utilized to gain access to the rare, and therefore valuable, birds. The radio transmitters had been removed from the parrots and left in a pile outside the enclosure, and somehow the microchips had also been disabled.

The article stated the theft was apparently the work of professionals who had considerable knowledge of the kakapo's anatomy and characteristics and that they had pulled off the mission in an almost militarily precise manner. These were not run-of-the-mill thieves the authorities were dealing with. A substantial supply of specially formulated pellets used for supplemental feedings had also been filched by the parrot-nabbers. The heist had been extremely well planned.

I began to piece all my bits of knowledge together and realized Boris Dack was apparently a middleman in some kind of endangered parrot–trafficking ring. Shorty, the six o'clock caller, must have been one of the men involved in the actual abduction of the kakapos, and their destination was the personal zoo on the estate owned by Pablo Pikstone.

I printed off the media release and rushed downstairs to find Stone. I knew he'd be as flabbergasted and confused as I was. Stone was in the parlor with Robert Fischer discussing the snow, which was now coming down at a brisk rate and beginning to pile up on the grass. It was still melting on the sidewalk from the heat of the day radiating out of the concrete. As the temperature began to drop, the melted snow would quickly turn to ice, Robert Fischer predicted. Stone agreed with the amicable gentleman.

To explain to Stone what I'd discovered, I joined in their conversation and waited until after Robert Fischer had bidden us good night and retired to his room. Midway through reading the news release I'd handed him, Stone asked, "Basil, Gunner, Bella and Maggie? They all have names? Aren't they wild parrots? This sounds a little personal."

"Yes, but according to the web page, the DOC staff has named each of them for easier identification. I'm sure the staff members are similar to doting mother hens, watching over their brood. It would be natural for them to name the chicks as they're hatched. From what I've read, every successful hatchling is a major feat. According to all I read, the mortality rate among these birds is extremely high."

"This is a big deal, isn't it?" Stone was just beginning to understand the enormity of the situation. "I guess it's not just your everyday case of bird-napping, as I'd first thought. That is, if there is such a thing as an everyday bird-napping."

"I'm afraid it's not a typical occurrence. I think we need to alert the authorities so they can set up a sting operation of some type. They'd only need to arrange a stake-out on Boris, tail him to the transfer site tomorrow night, and catch him in the act of turning over the kakapos to Mr. Pikstone."

"Okay. It's too late tonight, but I will go down to the police station in the morning, or at least talk with someone there. They can determine who to contact, and what actions to take. Good work, Lexie. I still believe hiding under Boris's bed was a foolish and ill-advised act on your part, but I can't deny it may turn out to have been a fortuitous one, at least for the four threatened birds. Please don't attempt something that risky again. Okay?"

"Yes, well, I hope they can catch Mr. Pikstone, Boris, Shorty, and any other accomplices red-handed. I can't even imagine why someone would go to all that trouble and expense to steal endangered parrots."

"It's probably because of the novelty of owning something so rare, I'd guess," Stone said. "Pablo Pikstone can buy anything he wants, which probably makes him crave things that are more of a challenge to obtain. Something like four of the last eighty-six kakapos on the planet would be a real addition to his rare and exotic wildlife collection. You'd have to admit he'd probably be the first one on his block to own four—or even just a pair—of the kakapos. He might be hoping to mate and raise more of them himself, as a challenge of sorts. Stranger things have happened, I suppose."

"I suppose you're right, but it's a real shame to threaten the survival of the parrots the way he has. I'm sure the trauma of the capture and the long trip to America has not been easy on them."

"No, probably not," Stone said. "But hopefully, they'll all survive the ordeal and be returned safely to the DOC staff on Chalky or Codfish Island. Parrots in general have very long life spans, or so I've read. That probably indicates they are hardy creatures. Why don't you go on up to my suite, take a nice long bath, and get ready for bed, Lexie? I'll lock up down here and see that all of the guests are safely ensconced in their rooms, and then I'll be up in a few minutes."

"Okay, Stone. A nice long bath does sound very inviting."

I was looking forward to that long, hot soak in the tub as I walked up the stairs to the second floor. And I was looking forward to spending the night with Stone. There was little else on my mind as I climbed to the top of the staircase. I noticed it was pitch black in the hallway at the top of the landing. Hadn't I left the hall lights on when I'd come downstairs? Perhaps a guest had flicked the light switch off out of habit on the way to his room. I didn't give the matter any further thought.

As I approached the top step, I reached out to feel for the light switch. Instead I felt the warm skin of someone else's arm, just as a forceful shove sent me tumbling backwards down the stairs. My own arms were flailing about as my rear end bounced off one step after another. Fortunately, my hands were free, and I was finally able to grab the banister about halfway down, which kept me from tumbling all the way to the bottom of the steps. My backside had suffered the brunt of the abuse. For once I was thankful to have a little extra padding there.

As I began my descent down the stairs, I'd hollered out in surprise and alarm. Within seconds of my body coming to a stop, sprawled out midway down the staircase, Stone appeared at my side and began examining me for signs of injury. Before long, most of the guests, in various stages of undress, were huddled around me, watching silently as Stone felt for broken bones. Satisfied that I was still in one piece, he asked me what had happened to cause my fall.

"Somebody pushed me!" I looked suspiciously at the crowd around me.

I heard a collective gasp among the guests, and I tried to determine who was not present among the group. Only Rosalinda Swift and Boris Dack were missing, I concluded. Everyone else was gathered around me, staring with stunned expressions, and waiting for me to continue with my story.

"Just as I reached the top of the staircase and was searching for the light switch, I felt the arm of someone standing there. Then I was shoved backwards. I tried to grab hold of the arm I'd felt but failed. He stepped back as he shoved me, I believe."

"Who was it?" Harry Turner asked. "Couldn't you see the person at all?"

"No, I don't know who it was," I said, shrugging. I winced as a sharp pain shot from my shoulder down to the tips of my fingers. "With the lights out, it was too dark to see anything at the top of the stairs."

"Where are you hurting?" Stone asked. "I don't feel any broken bones, at least. Still, it might be a good idea to take you to the ER and have you examined and x-rayed."

"I don't think that's necessary. They might get tired of seeing me at the ER if I make a habit of going there every night. I banged my head pretty hard a couple times, and my shoulder feels like it was pulled out of its socket when I grabbed the banister. But other than that and a few nasty bruises, I should be okay. I was lucky, I guess."

"You were *very* lucky, little lady," Cornelius said, standing beside me in ridiculous-looking white silk pajamas, dotted with small red hearts. He had a smug look on his face. He winked at me as he slightly jutted his pelvis out. Good Lord, did he think he was the personification of sex appeal?

"He's right," Stone said. "You could've been seriously injured. As it is, you're going to be very sore for a few days. You are going to take it easy for awhile, even if Crystal and I have to tie you to the bed."

Stone picked me up gingerly and carried me back up the stairs. One of the guests had flipped on the light before coming down to see what the commotion was all about. Stone turned slightly to his left to address the crowd, still huddled together on the lower steps. It was obvious the events of the last two days were beginning to take a toll on them. Suddenly they seemed unable to think for themselves. They stood still, as if unable to move without permission from Stone, the man they were beginning to think of as their leader.

"I think it'd be best if you all went back to your rooms now," Stone said. "Thanks for your concern. I'll take care of Lexie now. Lock your doors, of course, but rest assured no one is going to bother any of you overnight."

The group slowly disbursed, and we could hear them muttering about the perils of staying at the Alexandria Inn as they made their way back to their rooms. It was obvious to me they were having difficulty believing they'd be safe in their rooms. I couldn't say I felt completely safe either, even as Stone carried me into his room and placed me on top of his massive king-sized bed.

"I'll start your bath water, honey. I'm glad we'd decided to have you stay in here with me tonight. There's no damned way I'd leave you alone in your room now. I don't want to let you out of my sight."

"Who could've pushed me, Stone? And why? I wish I'd gotten a look at him, but it was so dark, and I was taken completely off-guard."

"Anyone could've done it, I suppose. But why is someone so intent on causing you harm? I don't know what to think. But I do know I don't like it. I've just decided to take you back to your own house in Shawnee tomorrow. And I'm going to call Wendy and ask if she can be sure to stay with you for a couple of days while you recuperate. If nothing else, she can at least check in on you periodically during the day, and I'll do the same. You'll be safe there, and that's all that matters at this point."

"But—"

"My decision is firm. There'll be no debate about it. As long as we're involved with each other, I'm going to take care of you and protect you as best I can, whether you like it or not. So you might as well get used to it!"

Get used to it? No problem there. Having a handsome, thoughtful man take care of me, protect me, and worry about my safety was definitely something I could get used to. With a contented smile on my face, I closed my eyes and Stone unfolded a quilt at the foot of his bed and placed it over me. "Now I'm going to draw you a bath, complete with soft music, lighted, cucumber-melon scented candles, and those dissolving lavender oil beads you like so much. Holler if you need anything. I'll be back to get you in a couple of minutes."

By the time Stone returned from the bathroom to inform me my water was ready, I had fallen into a light, fitful sleep. I was barely conscious of Stone as he removed my socks and shoes, loosened my clothes, tucked the quilt around me again, and removed his own clothes to take advantage of the tub full of warm, scented water.

I could soak when I arose in the morning, and I needed the rest more than anything, I'm sure those were his thoughts as he let me sleep off the after effects of a rough day.

CHAPTER FOURTEEN

"Wake up, sleeping beauty," were the next words I heard. I felt a warm hand brushing the hair away from my face as I slowly opened my eyes. Stone was gazing at me with concern. There were deep creases around his eyes as he looked down at me. He was holding a tray laden with a heaping platter of food and a steaming cup of coffee. "I've brought you some breakfast, honey. How are you feeling today?"

"Good morning. It looks and smells delicious, Stone. Thank you. I feel a mite rough around the edges, but pretty good, considering the circumstances."

"Moving around just a bit might take away some of the stiffness, and eating will help you get some of your strength back. The breakfast is compliments of Crystal. It was her idea, and she made it for you after she finished cleaning the kitchen following the meal she cooked for the guests. She's cooked you crisp bacon, French toast, and two eggs, over hard. Ah, and here's an English muffin with strawberry jam."

"How sweet. She prepared all my favorites. She is such a sweetheart."

"Yes. She asked me what I thought you'd like best. She really is a sweet, thoughtful gal. And she doesn't seem to mind the thought of another long day of work catering to all these quirky old blue-haired, Historical Society nuts."

"They're still here?" I hoped I didn't sound as disenchanted by the news as I felt. After all, it wasn't as if the inn had suddenly been invaded by a swarm of twenty-pound subterranean termites. "Haven't all the guests been released to leave this morning? Last night they were all talking about going home today."

"Yes, but you haven't taken a look outside yet," Stone said. He walked over to the window and drew open the drapes as if revealing the most hideous sight imaginable. "Nothing is working in our favor this week, is it?"

All I could see when he opened the drapes was a wall of solid white out the window. There was a plain, old-fashioned blizzard taking place outdoors. "Holy moly," I exclaimed. "It must have snowed all night!"

"It's a winter wonderland out there, that's for sure," Stone said. He'd managed to make *winter wonderland* sound like a purgatory in hell. "There's nearly a foot of heavy, wet snow on the ground, and another two or three inches are expected. It's still coming down pretty fast and furious right now. Except in extreme emergencies, the sheriff's department has prohibited all travel. In fact, if you get stuck and don't have chains on your tires, you could be ticketed. None of the guests seemed too upset about being forced to spend another day here at my expense. They seem content to be waited on and fed and pampered like world renowned dignitaries while they wait out the storm."

"Oh, I can well imagine. How did Crystal get here this morning? I had promised to pick her up if the weather was bad."

"She called early this morning. I took your Jeep to St. Joseph at six-thirty and brought her back. I considered a house full of demanding old fogies an 'extreme emergency,' and thought it was worth the risk of getting stuck in your four-by-four to bring Crystal to the inn. I wouldn't have even scoffed at a hefty fine had I gotten stuck and ticketed. I might've even encouraged them to throw me in jail overnight," Stone said.

"Don't even think about it, Buster. You're not getting out of this that easily."

"No, I'm never that lucky. I told Crystal to bring an overnight bag so we wouldn't have to try to get her home this evening. The roads may be officially closed by then. She can use your room downstairs, since you won't be needing it."

"Good idea, I wish we'd thought of that last night." I took a few sips of my favorite espresso Stone had brought me. I noticed he was eyeing me intently, trying to judge my condition. I tried to force a measure of cheerfulness in my demeanor to ease his concern. "Any problems getting around in the snow with my Jeep?"

"None at all. Better start eating before your food gets cold."

"Okay. What time is it?"

"About a quarter after ten."

"It's after ten? I haven't slept that late in ages. Good Lord, Stone, why didn't you get me up earlier? I feel like the laziest slug alive."

"I thought the rest would be good for you. And with Crystal here, I didn't feel it was necessary to have you downstairs working in the kitchen. I knew she and I could take care of the guests adequately. Everyone's had breakfast and they're all milling around in the parlor, taking it easy this morning. A number of them are playing cards. They all seem to be in good spirits, at least."

"That's nice," I said. I took another long swallow of the espresso. I felt like I hadn't had a sip of coffee in days.

"I made an announcement at breakfast that, due to the accident you endured last night, there'll be no maid service today. Crystal can only do so much, and since this entire scenario was unforeseen, I'm counting on the guests to make their beds and tidy up their own rooms today. Crystal will be busy enough just keeping them fed."

"Good for you! There's no sense letting them work Crystal to the bone. Keeping Patty Poffenbarger fed could be a full-time job all by itself."

"That's what I thought, too. I'm sure cleaning up after themselves while they're guests at the inn might be considered a real imposition to several of them, but, amazingly, no one complained about my announcement. When I passed through the parlor a few minutes ago, they were setting up two card tables and choosing up teams for their game of pitch. Alma Turner was going into the kitchen to help Crystal make another pot of coffee, and Patty Poffenbarger was sweeping the front entryway while Otto was outside shoveling the sidewalk. I made him quit, however, because men our age have a tendency to drop over dead from heart attacks caused by the exertion of shoveling. I hired that redheaded young man up the street, named Walter Sneed, to come down and clear the sidewalks. So, as you can see, things are going along just fine, even while you lounge around like a lazy slug, as you put it."

"That's a relief. I still feel guilty lying in bed while you and Crystal are working."

"Well, don't! Now you finish up your breakfast. You're not going to get away with just drinking coffee, so you might as well dig in. While you eat I'm going to draw you another bath. It might make you feel a little perkier. I ended up using the last bath I drew for you to wash my own tired body."

"I'm sorry, I didn't mean—"

"Don't be sorry. I was glad to see you could fall asleep. You needed the rest. And I rather enjoyed those lavender oil beads and scented candles. Although, I have to admit, I found myself wishing I had a little curly-haired, brown-eyed beauty to share them with me." Stone was teasing, but I knew he'd been looking forward to a little romance and intimacy last night. I'd been looking forward to the same things. I vowed to make it up to him, and it was a promise I'd enjoy fulfilling.

After Stone started the water running in the tub, he ducked his head around the corner and said, "Since it's no longer possible for you to go home as I'd planned, I want you to be extra cautious today. In fact, I'd prefer you kept yourself locked in my suite as much as possible, away from the guests. You can read, watch television, surf the Internet on my computer, or just lounge around in bed. No talking to guests or wandering around the inn. Okay? I won't be able to keep an eye on you all day."

"Oh, all right," I said. "But only because I don't want you to worry about me, and it's obvious someone here is determined to give you cause to worry."

"And they're succeeding. Maybe you can get those featherbed mattresses ordered for me today. Fire up my computer and do a little Internet surfing."

"Okay, that's a good idea."

"Oh, and by the way, I offered to loan your Jeep to Boris. He told me he was desperate to attend a vitally important meeting that's scheduled for six o'clock this evening, and he was concerned about how he'd get to it. I acted like I had no idea what the six o'clock meeting was about and told him I knew you'd be happy to lend him your vehicle, which is so reliable in the snow. You don't mind, do you? I thought it was important he didn't miss the scheduled rendezvous with Mr. Pikstone."

"You're exactly right. It's the perfect solution, actually. My Jeep will be easy to tail. It practically glows in the dark. And I won't be in need of it this evening, anyway. Did you get in touch with the authorities on the kakapo abduction? Or has somebody who can contact the authorities been told about it?"

"Well, I wasn't sure who to contact, so I called the Rockdale Police Department and talked to Wyatt—Detective Johnston—and he said he'd talk to Sergeant O'Brien and have O'Brien contact the New Zealand Department of Conservation and whatever authorities he thought needed to be informed about the situation. Nevertheless, it's in their hands now, and he assured me there'd be arrests made at the transfer tonight. He promised to call me later on today with an update."

"Good. I'm anxious to see how it turns out. And I can rest easy today, knowing something's being done to save the parrots," I said.

"Yes. We've done about all we can do. Wyatt couldn't help laughing about the situation when I explained it to him. He said it'd be the first parrot-napping case the Rockdale Police Department had ever been involved in."

"I can well imagine."

"Now, I want you to rest and enjoy your bath. Relax and try not to worry or be involved in anything that requires a trip to the ER tonight, okay? Boris will have your Jeep, and my Corvette is absolutely worthless on snow and ice."

I agreed to take it easy and do my best to stay out of trouble. After I polished off the entire tray of food, I took a long, much-needed, soak in the tub. My stiff, aching body was very appreciative. I still had a dull throb in my right temple where I'd struck the railing. I took a couple of ibuprofen tablets I'd brought along in my toiletry bag. Stone had transferred my toiletries and my garment bag from my former suite downstairs. I had every intention of lounging around all day, reading and resting, and staying out of harm's way. My good intentions lasted nearly a full hour.

CHAPTER FIFTEEN

I'd almost drifted off to sleep again when I heard a light, tentative tapping on my door. Out of habit, I glanced over at Stone's alarm clock and saw it was only eleven o'clock on this snowy Wednesday morning and already I was tired of lying around in bed. I put on Stone's plaid flannel robe and stepped into my own fuzzy slippers. There was another, more assertive, rap on the door, and I called out, "Who is it?"

I heard a muffled reply, which I didn't comprehend. I couldn't even distinguish whether it was a male or female voice that responded.

"Who?" I asked again.

"It's Rosalinda," I heard clearly this time, even though she spoke in a breathy whisper. "Rosalinda Swift. May I speak with you for a moment? Please? I won't keep you long."

I opened the door, and Rosalinda nearly fell into the room. I wasn't certain if she was already on her way to getting tipsy, or if she'd just been leaning against my door in order to hear my reply. Perhaps it was a little of both.

"Come on in," I said. Stone had cautioned me against speaking to any of the guests, but I didn't feel at all threatened by this older, limp-looking woman. I felt confident I could defend myself in the event of an unprovoked attack. Last evening she'd been too inebriated to climb the stairs, much less climb them and shove me back down them, so I didn't feel there was any chance she was behind the misdeeds taking place at the inn. It was fortunate for Rosalinda her room was on the first floor, or she'd never make it up to her bed after happy hour each evening. I motioned her into the room and closed the door behind her. "What's up, Rosalinda? What did you want to see me about?"

"Cornelius just told me what happened last night on the staircase, and I wanted to check and see how you were faring today. First the poisoning, and now this—on top of Horatio's murder—what in heaven's name is going on around here?"

"I don't know, but I wish I did," I said. "I am a little sore today from my tumble down the stairs last night, but otherwise I'm doing fine."

"After that terrifying incident at supper, with Patty nearly choking to death, I felt a mite overwrought and decided to turn in early last night," Rosalinda said. She ran her hand over her calf-length skirt several times, as if trying to iron out an invisible wrinkle.

"I don't blame you. Did you sleep well?" I asked.

"No. I tossed and turned all night, but it's to be expected with all that's been happening here at the inn the last couple of days. Nothing personal, my dear, but sometimes I wonder why we even chose this inn for the induction in the first place. We would have been wise to pick accommodations with a long-standing reputation of professionalism."

"Um, yeah, whatever . . ."

"I was all set to go home this morning until this blizzard struck. Even though I was disappointed to have my plans thwarted, I've always enjoyed watching it snow and can't help but think it's beautiful out—"

Okay, enough of this small talk, I thought. This vodka-swilling woman, who probably thinks I'm nothing more than a scullery maid, did not struggle up the stairs to check on my physical condition or tell me how much she adored snow. It was time to find out what she really wanted.

"So, what was it exactly you wanted to discuss with me, Ms. Swift?"

"Well, um, I'm aware of the fact you've been doing some snooping . . . er, I mean, investigating and inquiring as to who might be responsible for Mr. Prescott's murder, and I was hoping there was some way you could help my brother—"

"Your brother?"

"Uh, actually, he's my half-brother."

"Your half-brother?"

"Yes, and it's all my fault, I know," Rosalinda said. Her eyes began to well up with tears, and with trembling hands she reached into the cleavage of her silk blouse and pulled out a tissue the way a magician would extract a bunny rabbit from his top hat. She dabbed at her eyes and began to babble. "I don't know what to do. He's not the one behind all of this. It's entirely my fault. I should never have. But how was I to know. Oh my, you've just got to try to help him, Ms. Starr."

"Whoa there. Calm down Rosalinda, and tell me who your half-brother is and why he needs help. I'm afraid you've completely lost me."

"Peter Randall is my half-brother. We had the same mother, you see, and he's been arrested and charged with the murder of Horatio Prescott," Rosalinda said.

"Peter Randall's your half-brother? Hmm, that's interesting. Please go on."

"They've got the wrong man. My brother would never have taken another man's life. Not even Prescott's."

"How can you be so certain, Rosalinda? The authorities must be fairly convinced, or they wouldn't have arrested Peter for the crime. Your brother's alibi was pretty shaky, you know, and he did have a recent lawsuit filed against him by the victim. There seems to be a history of bad blood and a lot of friction and controversy between the two men. And, as you probably know, these are the kinds of things that add up to a strong motive for murder in the eyes of detectives."

"That's just not the case, though. The bad blood was between Horatio and me, not Horatio and Peter. Let me start at the beginning," Rosalinda said as she awkwardly sat her bony butt down on the edge of Stone's bed. She shook her head and let out a long, dramatic sigh.

"As I said, Peter and I shared the same mother. My mother married Stu Randall five years after my father died, and Peter was born about eleven months later. My stepfather, Stu, was killed by lightning in 1983 while playing on a golf course in Arizona.

"When our mother passed away in 1985, she willed the Victorian mansion in the Museum Hill district in St. Joseph to Peter and me. It's the home where Mother had lived her entire life. The home was called 'Lily Belle' after my great-great-grandmother, the original owner of the home. Therefore, Peter and I are the co-owners of the historic home, which is now completely restored and open to the public. I live in another historic home that I recently purchased here in Rockdale, just two blocks from my brother's home. I'm in the process of having it restored, as well, and it's more convenient to stay there while the restoration is taking place. By the way, Peter's a self-employed financial consultant here in town."

I nodded, and glanced up at the sound of my door creaking open. Crystal peered around it with a surprised expression. "Oh, uh, sorry. I didn't know anyone else was in here. Hello, Ms. Swift. Is everything okay, Lexie?" she asked me.

"Everything's fine, Crystal. Rosalinda and I are just chatting. And I owe you a huge thanks for that breakfast. It was terrific, sweetie."

Crystal smiled and asked me if I wanted another cup of coffee. She was balancing a carafe of a Colombian blend on a round serving tray. It wasn't espresso, but even a cup of regular coffee sounded appealing to me. I sniffed appreciatively at the fragrant aroma as she filled my cup. Nothing was as welcome to me in the morning as the scent of fresh coffee.

There was a clean, empty cup on Crystal's tray that she filled for Rosalinda. Without having to ask, Crystal automatically dropped two sugar cubes and a dollop of cream into Rosalinda's coffee, and stirred it several times before handing the cup to the older woman.

"Thank you," Rosalinda said. She blew on the edge of her cup and took a small sip. "It's perfect—as usual."

"You're welcome. Let me know if you need anything, Lexie," Crystal said. As she slipped out the door, she left it noticeably ajar. I appreciated the young woman's show of concern and caution. She had no way of knowing whether or not Rosalinda Swift posed any danger to me. All the guests seemed harmless, but one of them wasn't as benign as he appeared. There was at least one book staying here that couldn't be judged by its cover, I realized. I couldn't let myself lose sight of that fact and become careless. After Crystal had departed, I prompted Rosalinda to continue.

"So, anyway, I wanted to keep Lily Belle in the family, but Peter wanted to sell the home. It's worth a great deal of money, you know. And we've bickered about this all these years since Mother died. I just can't stand the thought of some outsider owning Lily Belle, the home I grew up in and loved dearly my entire life."

"I can understand why you'd be so sentimental about the place," I said. "But I can see Peter's side of it, too. I imagine it is a lot to keep up."

"Yes, it certainly can be nearly a full-time job and a great deal of expense. I'm beginning to understand his feelings about selling the place, also." Rosalinda continued to recite the rest of her story as if it was something she wasn't happy about disclosing. "Well, as I was saying, a year or so before Mother was diagnosed with liver disease, I was engaged to the late Mr. Prescott. Yes, we were lovers, believe it or not. But, I'm sorry to say, the relationship came to an abrupt end, and I was crushed. If we'd just broken up and gone our separate ways, it would've been one thing, but instead, he tarnished my reputation and made me a laughing stock among my peers, and that was unforgivable. I was humiliated in front of my family and friends."

"Oh? How'd he tarnish your reputation?" I asked. "How'd he humiliate you?"

"He insinuated I was only interested in him for his money and made comments to that effect all over town. I'll admit I did have a lot of debts, due to high restoration expenses at Lily Belle mainly, but I would've never lowered myself to marry merely for money. Never! I truly loved the arrogant ass, or at least I thought I did. But I vowed that one day I'd make Horatio regret having sullied my good name in public the way he did. I was determined to even the score and have the last laugh. And it took a long, long time, but eventually I did!'"

"Oh, my God! So it was you who killed him?" I asked, nearly gasping in shock. I couldn't hide my surprise or my disapproval. I glanced up to verify the door was still ajar in the event Rosalinda felt obliged to shoot me in the head with a small handgun she had concealed in her cleavage, after she'd finished her confession.

"No, no, of course not, Ms. Starr. Don't be silly. I didn't want to see Horatio dead. I wanted to see him knocked off his high horse, so to speak. Publicly humiliated, as I'd been. But I certainly didn't want him killed. After all, there's no fun or satisfaction in humiliating a dead man. I wanted to see him sweat."

"Oh, well, that's a relief," I said. My heart felt as if it was racing. "So, what *did* you do? How did you knock him off that high horse?"

"I made a deal with my brother," Rosalinda said, nearly under her breath. I had to lean forward and ask her to repeat herself, which she did reluctantly.

"I made a deal with Peter. If he'd engineer a plan that succeeded in bringing about considerable financial ruin to Horatio Prescott, I would agree to sell the Lily Belle so he could cash out his half of the estate. He declined my offer—again and again—until, finally, one day he agreed to encourage Horatio to invest heavily in a high-tech computer software company, the hottest new IPO on the NASDAQ. Peter had just received inside information regarding the company's finances. The company had become too big too fast and had bit off more than it could conceivably chew. Peter heard, from a reliable source inside the company, that the CEOs of the corporation were planning to liquidate and file Chapter Seven bankruptcy in the near future.

"Peter told Horatio instead that the company was about to be bought out by Microsoft, and the stockholders would realize a huge profit. Horatio, naturally, rushed to jump on the bandwagon, invested heavily, and ultimately lost over half his net worth. It was the retribution I'd prayed for all those years. The only thing that would've brought me more satisfaction is if I could have somehow let him know I was responsible for his misfortune. But, of course, this was impossible, for my own safety, of course.

"I felt justice had been served, however, and Peter's end of the bargain had been kept, so I placed the Lily Belle on the market, as promised. I currently have several potential buyers interested in purchasing the property. Due to the lawsuit Prescott had recently filed against Peter, it now appears to the authorities as if Peter had an intense hatred of Prescott and a fervent motive to kill him. But Peter would never have murdered him. It's not in his nature to physically harm anyone, and especially not Prescott. My brother wanted his half of the money from the Lily Belle too much to kill him. He knew I'd never uphold my end of the bargain if anything happened to Prescott."

Rosalinda finally took a break from her recital. With a deep breath, she studied my face in an attempt to judge my reaction to her story. I believed her. I couldn't imagine anyone would make up a story like that. But I wasn't sure what she thought I could do to help her brother. I expressed my desire to see her brother cleared of the murder. What he'd done was morally, if not legally, wrong, but it wasn't murder. He shouldn't be held responsible for murder in the first degree if he was only guilty of a lesser crime. And shouldn't some of the responsibility of this lesser crime ultimately land in Rosalinda's lap?

I instinctively knew from the beginning Peter Randall wasn't the killer. I knew for a fact he didn't poison me, and Peter didn't push me down the stairs, and I would bet whoever had done those things had also shot Horatio. I couldn't live with myself if I just sat back and let an innocent man be held responsible for a murder he didn't commit while the actual killer walked around as a free man. I had to at least attempt to do something to clear Peter Randall's name so the authorities would get back to the matter of finding and bringing the real killer to justice.

"How can I help him? What can I do?" I asked Rosalinda.

"I don't know, Ms. Starr. I was hoping you'd have an idea."

I was afraid of that. "Where is Peter now?" I asked.

"I imagine he's at home, due to the winter storm. Of course, he works out of his home the majority of the time, anyway. He has an office there and another one in a business building downtown. I can call and find out if he's at home."

"So he's not in jail awaiting arraignment?"

"No, I guess there wasn't strong enough evidence to hold him without bond. He'll plead not guilty, naturally, but I worry his alibi is so weak they'll manage to hang him with the murder, anyway. If Peter said he was at the movies, then I know that's where he was, regardless of whether or not he recognized all the actors or was recognized himself by the theatre's employees. Is there some way you can prove he was at the theatre that night? Is there anything at all you can do that might help?"

She was beginning to sound desperate, but I didn't want to promise anything I had no prayer of delivering. Still, I felt a sense of responsibility to try to help. I needed to do something, even if, in the end, it proved to be a lesson in futility.

"Is your brother married?"

"He's a widower. His wife June died of lymphoma many years ago, and he's been alone ever since."

"Okay. Tell me Peter's address, and I'll go talk to him. Don't call him. I don't want him to know I'm coming or that I've spoken with you. For now, I think it's best to keep your name out of it. Agreed?"

"Yes, I'd feel better if he didn't know I asked you to help him."

"I don't expect to be gone any longer than an hour, and my Jeep will get through this snow just fine. I promised to loan the Jeep to Boris Dack this evening, but I'll be back in plenty of time for that. It's sure handy owning a four-wheel drive vehicle. In fact, I could probably deliver you to your home, which would give me an excuse to be out and about in this storm. You said you had some pressing reason to leave this morning, didn't you?"

"Well—I—uh—no, not really. Actually, I'd prefer to stay so I can take my car home with me when I leave," Rosalinda said. "Tomorrow will be soon enough to go home."

What happened to being disappointed at having her plans

thwarted? I wondered.

"Oh, all right. But Stone is not going to be happy with me if he notices I'm gone. I practically promised him I'd stay in bed and rest all day. So I'll need you to help cover for me, okay?"

"Okay. What do you have in mind? I'll help any way I can."

"Give me about ten minutes to get ready," I said. "Then find Stone and tell him you and I just had a nice chat. Tell him you left when you saw I was having trouble staying awake. He'll assume I'm sleeping and not want to bother me. Try to keep him away from the front windows and distracted long enough for me to back my Jeep down the driveway and up the street."

"All right."

"If Stone seems concerned, try to get Crystal to confirm that you and I were having a pleasant conversation when she popped in with the coffee."

I had the feeling there'd be hell to pay later, but I sometimes think it's easier to ask for forgiveness than for permission.

"Would it be all right with you if I enlisted Cornelius's help in detaining Stone? He'd be able to distract him easier than I because he's such a—"

"Pervert?" I asked.

"—beguiling character."

Did I hear right? Did she say "beguiling character?" Did people actually use the word "beguiling" anymore? She was half-right, I concluded. Cornelius was, without doubt, a character. Rosalinda had not heard my own one-word, less-complimentary depiction of Cornelius, as she continued on with her own flattering description of the man. I was starting to feel nauseated, as if breakfast hadn't settled quite right.

"And he's such a brilliant conversationalist, don't you think? The handsome devil is so charming and witty, and just brimming with all that natural charisma—"

The over-imbibing was clearly rendering Rosalinda Swift

clueless. It was almost enough to make me want to rush home and throw out whatever remained in my bottle of Kahlua and the three remaining Key Lime wine coolers in my fridge. It occurred to me that Rosalinda was not concerned about leaving her car at the inn, but rather about leaving the "handsome devil" behind.

"Having Cornelius help would be fine, Rosalinda. But we must not let it go any further than the three of us," I said.

"All right, Lexie. I give you my word. Thank you for helping me and my brother, Peter. After Cornelius and I detain Stone long enough for you to slip out, I think I'll go to the parlor and look for something to drink for lunch."

CHAPTER SIXTEEN

The snow was deeper and tougher to navigate than I'd anticipated. The state plows were concentrating on clearing the snow off the major thoroughfares and leaving the residential streets until last. It took three attempts to drive my Jeep through the drift at the end of the driveway. I began to doubt my wisdom in even attempting to drive across town. I felt warm and flushed; a hot flash no doubt.

Nearly a half hour passed before I reached Peter Randall's house, an all-brick ranch in a middle-class neighborhood. His corner house was directly across from the commercial district. I could see a strip shopping mall, an all-night diner, and a movie theatre. I was forced to park in the middle of the street due to the depth of snow along the curb.

I'd seen almost no traffic the entire way over, and I doubted I'd be blocking anyone's path in the next ten or fifteen minutes. That was the maximum time I intended to stay, anyway. I left the Jeep running so it'd be warm inside when I got back and made my way down an unshoveled sidewalk to the icy steps leading up to Peter's front door. The intensity of the snow had increased. I could barely see three feet before me as I held tightly to the railing and climbed the steps of his tiny front porch.

The weary-looking gentleman who answered the door didn't look like a killer. He looked like a defeated, remorseful man facing a firing squad. He had a badly fitted hairpiece lying askew on top of his head. He wore expensive but old-fashioned slacks and a sleeveless white t-shirt, the type my father had always jokingly referred to as a "wife-beater," for some reason that's still unclear to me. Nevertheless, it was obvious Peter Randall hadn't expected company in the midst of the worst blizzard of the season.

"Yes?" he asked, as he opened the door.

"Mr. Randall?"

"Yes, I'm Peter Randall. Can I help you? Is your vehicle stuck?" he asked. He sounded convinced no one would be calling at his house except to borrow his phone to make an emergency phone call.

"Hi, I'm Stacey Shryock, and no, I'm not stuck. I came to see you, hoping to hire you as my financial advisor."

"Today? In this storm?" It was evident in his voice he thought my request was absurd.

"Well, yes," I said. I hadn't given the bizarreness factor of my ruse much thought. It was time to punt, as I frequently found myself in need of doing. "Because of the weather, I had the day off work, and figured it'd be a good day to see you without a prior appointment. My Jeep was designed for extreme weather like this, and I thought I'd take advantage of the fact."

"I see." The look on his face made it clear that what he saw was a deranged ninny.

"I see," he said again. He looked up at my Jeep, still idling in the middle of the street. "Guess you better come on in, Ms. Shryock, and get in out of the cold."

I followed Mr. Randall to a small room in the rear of the home. Mr. Randall was an immaculate housekeeper, I noticed. I doubted there was a single dust mote in the entire house. By the smell of Lysol in the air, I'd caught him in the act of disinfecting something. Was a house this clean a sign of a meticulous mind—a beneficial trait for a financial advisor—or a sign of an obsessive/compulsive disorder? I had to admit I'd feel a little more at ease if I spotted a cobweb in the corner of the ceiling, or a smudgy fingerprint on the plate-glass window. At least I'd feel more at home, anyway.

Once we'd settled into a couple of chairs in his home office, I began lying through my teeth. I explained to him I was expecting a substantial windfall soon, an inheritance from a great aunt, on her deathbed, of course. I was very saddened by Auntie Lou's imminent passing but wanted to be prepared to handle the large sum of money she'd allocated for me in her will. The least I could do was to invest my inheritance wisely so I'd have a nest egg to fall back on in difficult times.

I needed someone like Mr. Randall who could map out a wise investment course for me. As he responded to my plea, I could tell Mr. Randall was pleased at the opportunity to impress me with his financial expertise.

"Are you looking for a long-term investment, such as an individual retirement account?" he asked. "Do you prefer safe, lower-yielding investments, like certificates of deposit or municipal bonds? Or are you, perhaps, looking for a higher rate of return on your money? Something a little riskier, but with greater earnings potential, in which case, we'd want to consider a mutual fund or stock in some blue chip companies." I noticed while he spoke he was repeatedly rubbing his eyes, which were red and puffy. "There are a number of stocks that fall into this category. I could highly recommend a few of them for you."

"Uh, I'll need to consider all the options. Maybe I should think about investing a portion into each of the different options."

"That's actually what I was about to suggest, Ms. Shryock. It's never wise to put all your eggs in one basket, as I'm sure you've heard before. The smartest choice would be to diversify your portfolio." His eyes were beginning to water and tears were spilling over and running down the sides of his cheeks. He patted them with a handkerchief he'd pulled out of his top drawer.

"Are you all right, Mr. Randall?" I asked.

"Uh-huh."

"Have I come at a bad time?"

"No, my eyes are just bothering me today. Could you please excuse me for a few minutes, Ms. Shryock? My contacts must be dirty or scratched or something. They're really aggravating my eyes, even more than usual. I'm beginning to think I may have developed an allergy of some kind. I hope you won't mind if I go and remove them?"

"Of course not. I'm in no particular hurry." I wanted to sustain the impression I thought this the perfect day to be out and about, running errands and hiring new financial advisors.

"There's a fresh pot of coffee in the kitchen if you'd like to help yourself," Mr. Randall said, standing up to leave the room. "The kitchen is right down the hall, and there are clean cups in the cabinet right above the coffee maker. I'll just be a minute or two."

Coffee sounded good, as was normally the case with me, even when it was weak as I expected that Mr. Randall's would be. I was eager to see if his kitchen was a spotless as his office and living room. I wasn't surprised to find that it was. It looked as if it had never been cooked or eaten in. It had a rather depressing look to it.

I was sipping on my surprisingly stout coffee when Mr. Randall returned to his tidy, little office, wearing large, dark-rimmed glasses. I noticed with amusement he'd slipped a fitted sweater over the "wife-beater" muscle shirt he'd been wearing earlier. His toupee had been straightened, as well.

"Feel better?" I asked.

"Yes, much better, thanks."

"I've tried, but never could become accustomed to wearing

contacts. I finally decided it wasn't worth the hassle when I primarily only needed corrective lenses for driving, to correct a slight nearsightedness," I said.

"Contacts can take some getting used to. I've been having a lot of trouble with them lately because I think they're scratched and need to be replaced with new ones. I guess I need to make an appointment with the ophthalmologist to have my vision rechecked, or at least order new contacts. I'd like to try the kind you can leave in for days at a time. I have to take my current pair out every night."

"Yes, you should have your eyes examined regularly," I agreed. "Your vision is nothing to mess around with," I said. Good advice from a lady who has her eyes examined on an every-other-decade basis, and a routine physical every five or six years, whether she needed one or not. I'd always been much better at maintaining my vehicles than I was at maintaining my body.

I changed the subject quickly, as I needed to be on my way home before Stone realized I wasn't napping in his room at the inn. "You sure do look familiar to me, Mr. Randall. Do you belong to the country club?"

"No."

"Do you golf at all?"

"Haven't picked up a club in years, Ms. Shryock."

"Were you at the horse races the other evening?"

"No."

"Hmm. Were you, by chance, at the theatre the other night when they showed the movie, *Oh, God!* at the dollar show?"

"Yes, as a matter of fact, I was!" Peter nearly shouted at me.

"That's it, then."

"Yes, I was there that night. You must have seen me there," he said. He was obviously taken aback by my last question. He sat up straighter and looked at me with new interest. I knew he was wondering if I was someone who could corroborate his alibi. "I was sitting in the back row, on the far end. There was no one else in the row."

"Uh-huh, that's right. I remember now. You were sitting by yourself on the back row, which is exactly where I saw you. I knew you looked familiar, but for a minute, I just couldn't recall where it was I'd seen you before."

"Well, I'm sorry I don't recognize you, too, but I slept through the entire movie, I think. The young usher boy had to wake me up to tell me to go home after the movie had ended," Peter said.

"Oh, that's okay. I really couldn't expect you to remember seeing me in a dark theatre. I just have this thing about faces. I wish I could remember people's names as well as I do their faces. If you were so tired, why did you go to the movies in the first place?"

"I've been under a lot of stress recently. There are many unexpected complications in my life right now, and insomnia has been a severe problem the last few weeks," Peter said.

I nodded and said, "I have trouble with insomnia, too."

"I couldn't get to sleep on Sunday night," Peter continued. "I finally gave up and walked over to the picture show directly across the street from here, you know. I'm not a movie-person as a rule, but I thought it might take my mind off more pressing matters and help me relax. I hadn't expected it to relax me to the point I'd fall sound asleep in my seat. But I hadn't had a good night's sleep in weeks, and that's exactly what happened. I'm very glad you saw me there."

"You are? Why?" I didn't want to let on that I knew about Mr. Randall's recent arrest for suspicion of murder. News of the arrest hadn't yet made the front page of the *Rockdale Gazette,* as far as I knew, and as Stacey Shryock, it'd be easy to assume I'd have no knowledge of his connection to the recent local homicide victim.

"It may help me out with one of the little problems I've recently experienced. I know this is a strange request to make, Ms. Shryock, but would you mind signing a statement that you remember seeing me at the theatre Sunday night?" Peter asked anxiously.

"What?" I said, with the most perplexed expression I could muster. My limited acting experience, small roles in school plays during high school, was coming in handy.

Mr. Randall's request was reasonable, but it was impossible for me to sign a statement indicating I'd seen him at the local movie theatre Sunday night because there wasn't a sliver of truth to it. And the Rockdale detectives would know it was untrue. They knew I was lying in bed just nine feet below the victim, as he was being slain by an unknown executioner.

"It's a long story, Ms. Shryock," Peter Randall said. "But the gist of it is, I need someone to back up an affirmation I made stating I was at the theatre Sunday night and not somewhere else. It's the truth, as you know. I would never ask anyone to lie on my behalf. I just need someone like you to validate my statement for me."

"Couldn't the usher who woke you up at the end of the movie identify you and vouch for you?"

"No, apparently the kid can't remember me at all. Probably been smoking pot or something." Peter looked disgusted as he spoke.

"Hmm, I think I might be able to take care of the problem without even signing a statement."

"You can? How? I don't understand. Why would you do such a thing for me? How could you help when you don't really know me or the circumstances?"

"Don't worry," I said. "You'll just have to place blind trust in me for now. I'll try to get back in touch with you soon—about the investment portfolio as well as validating your claim to have been in the theatre."

I wasn't patronizing Peter. I really did intend to think about investing in a money market account. A few shares of Microsoft stock might be a wise investment, too. I wished I'd bought some shares of it several years back when I'd first considered it.

I sat my empty coffee cup on his desk, grabbed my coat off the chair's back, and made my way quickly to the front door with Peter Randall following closely on my heels. I was his ticket to exoneration, and he was understandably reluctant to let me out of his house and out of his sight. I was anxious to get over to the police station. I had a good idea what needed to be done to clear Peter Randall of the murder of Horatio Prescott III.

"Damn! Damn! Damn," I cursed, pounding my fists on the steering wheel. I'd been driving up Main Street on my way to the police station when my right front tire had swerved and slid off the pavement. The Jeep had come to a rest down in the ditch, axle-deep in heavy, wet snow.

I shifted the transfer case into four-wheel drive low, but the vehicle still refused to budge. I even tried wedging chunks of plywood under the tires and scattering cat litter and salt crystals all around the tires of the Jeep. All winter long I'd carried these items behind the rear seat for just this sort of emergency. I even had a bag of sand strategically placed over each of the rear wheel wells for traction. I might as well have been hauling around chocolate-covered raisins and old magazines. At least I'd have comfort food to munch on and something to read while I waited for help. Next winter, I vowed, my emergency survival kit would contain more logical and realistic items.

Finally, I accepted the fact I wasn't going to get the Jeep out of the ditch on my own, and I turned on my cell phone to call

Doug's Towing, the only wrecker company in Rockdale. I was hoping to be pulled out of the ditch and on my way to the police station before one of the local policemen came along and ticketed me for not having chains on my tires.

The man answering the phone at Doug's Towing told me there were two jobs in line ahead of me. Once he finished the job he was working on and towed another vehicle across town, he'd come and pull me out of the ditch. He estimated his arrival time at an hour to ninety minutes. I agreed to wait because I knew I had no other choice other than to call Stone, and that would be my very last resort.

I clipped the phone back on my belt and looked in my rearview mirror and was irked to see the reflection of a police car pulling up on the pavement beside me. I groaned and struck the steering wheel with the palm of my right hand again. "Damn! Damn! Damn!"

I groaned louder and added one more empathic "Damn!" when I saw Detective Wyatt Johnston step out of the patrol car. I knew there were several other officers on the police force in Rockdale. Couldn't it have been one of them instead of Johnston who just happened to drive down the street and find me in this predicament? Wyatt's eyebrows arched in surprise as he bent over and peered down into my window.

"Lexie? Is that you?"

"Yes, it's me. Hello there, Detective Johnston. I suppose you're going to ask me why I don't have chains on my tires and issue me a ticket."

"No, we rarely ever actually give out citations for motorists failing to have chains on their tires," he said with a laugh. "We only threaten to do it as a way of enticing them to stay off the streets until the snow plows can get them cleared off. What I really wanted to ask you is why you are out on the streets this morning to begin with. I know all about what's been going on at the inn and am surprised you are even out of bed. By the way, have you called anyone for assistance?"

"Doug's Towing. They said they'd be here in an hour or so."

"Okay, good. I just saw their tow truck pulling Howie Clamm out of the ditch in front of his house. He's the paper delivery guy for the *Rockdale Gazette*. Will you be all right here until the wrecker arrives? Have you got enough fuel?"

"Yes, I'll be fine, and my gas tank is over three-quarters full. I just noticed the Farm and Ranch Supply Store across the street. I need a couple of things they should carry, so I'll waste some time over there while I wait for the wrecker to arrive. But first, there's something important I need to tell you regarding the murder investigation. I was just heading to the police station when my tire slid off the pavement."

After discussing the homicide case with the detective for a few minutes, I thanked him for his help and climbed out of the Jeep. I hoped what I'd just related to him would help clear Peter Randall as a suspect, or at least give his story some credibility, by substantiating his claim he was at the movie theatre in the hours preceding Prescott's murder.

"Call and ask the dispatcher for me if you need anything," Wyatt Johnston said, pulling away from the curb. "I'll relay what you told me to Sergeant O'Brien. It makes perfect sense to me, Lexie."

I thanked him for his time and waved as he drove off. Then I locked the doors of the Jeep, although only someone with a tow truck could steal it, and made my way over to the Farm and Ranch store. I counted three vehicles there, in a parking lot that had seen only a rudimentary plowing. There were two SUVs and a large four-wheel drive pickup.

It soon became clear all three vehicles belonged to the help. I was probably the first customer to enter the store all morning. The older woman at the front desk greeted me like a long-lost friend and informed me only a skeleton crew was on hand at the store. She said most of the employees had been forced to stay home due to the blizzard conditions, but the floor clerk, Daphne, would be able to help me if I had any questions or problems.

"Speak of the devil," the lady said. "Here's comes Daphne now."

The young gal named Daphne was a Britney Spears look-alike. She smiled at me around the cherry lollipop she was sucking on. It was sticking out the corner of her mouth.

"Can I help you?" she asked after removing the sucker from her cheek, careful not to drop it. Daphne wore a pair of skin-tight blue jeans, riding so low on her hips that picking the lollipop up off the floor would have proved challenging and potentially revealing, if not physically impossible.

"I'm looking for tansy oil, Daphne. Do you carry it here?" I asked her.

"Is that the new skin-darkening cream? I've been wanting to try that, too," she said. Daphne was a true blonde, I could tell. "I hate lying out in the sun because it makes me all sweaty, and like, yucky."

"No, tansy oil has nothing to do with tanning."

"Oh? Then is it the stuff they put in chainsaws?"

"No, Daphne, they mix regular two-cycle motor oil in with the gasoline and put bar chain lube on the chain," I said. I felt like I was explaining trigonometry to a kindergartner. I was no chainsaw expert, but I felt like a member of Mensa talking to Daphne. "Actually, tansy oil is considered an herb—"

"Don't know nothing about herbs," she said, as she turned away, shrugging her bony shoulders.

"But, uh—"

"Sorry about that. I'll be back in the pet supplies department if you need me, Frieda." Daphne popped the sucker back into her beet-red mouth and walked away, her hips swaying back and forth.

The older woman had the decency to look embarrassed. "Youth," she said, a single word expressing a thorough explanation of the scene we'd just witnessed. "I'm sorry all of our department managers are off today. I'm Frieda Nihart, by the way. Feel free to look around in the herb department for the tansy oil while I search through our inventory list. I wish Mr. Walker were here today. I know he'd be able to help you. He seems to know a little about everything."

"Cornelius?" I asked.

"Yes, Cornelius Walker," Frieda said. "You must know him. Isn't he just the best thing to come along since Botox? All the customers flock to him for help and assistance. And all of the older single ladies just flock to him for the sake of being near him and to have a chance at maybe reeling him in. He'd be quite a catch, you know."

"So I've heard," I said, dryly. I studied Frieda's forehead for a second. If she was getting Botox treatments, it was a horrible waste of money on her part. She had furrows across her forehead you could plant potatoes in.

"Thank you, Frieda," I said, before heading back to the herb department. Was there something about Cornelius I'd overlooked? I wondered. Had my first impression of him clouded my ability to see him in a more realistic and favorable, light? I'd have to try to set my former opinions aside and re-evaluate him.

The store was eerily quiet. My footsteps seemed to echo as I walked down the aisle. I could even hear Daphne talking to a fish in an aquarium back in the pet department. "We'll find you a new home soon, my pretty little neon tetra," I heard her say. I couldn't hear if the neon tetra responded.

Looking around the herb department, I found nothing resembling tansy oil. I found about every other herb there was, and everything even remotely related to herbs and herb garden‑ing, but no tansy oil. Frieda joined me in a few minutes to tell me tansy oil was not listed in their inventory either, so she doubted the Farm and Ranch store had ever carried it. It would be a highly unlikely product for the store to carry, she told me.

I thanked her again, purchased a replacement tub of salt crystals and an ice scraper, and left the store. It was time to bite the bullet and call Stone. I had hoped it wouldn't come to this, but I really had no other option. Too much time had passed. He'd soon discover I wasn't in his room at the inn, if he didn't know already, and he'd be worried and upset. I wouldn't have been surprised to find Detective Johnston had already phoned Stone from his squad car.

Stone answered his cell phone on the first ring. "Lexie? Where are you? Are you all right?" There was anxiety in his voice, and I felt instantly contrite. I didn't deserve a man as understanding and thoughtful as Stone Van Patten.

"Yes, I'm okay. I apologize for sneaking out. There was something I really had to do, and I knew you'd balk at the idea of my leaving the inn," I said. I wiped my eyes with the sleeve of my jacket. I was perturbed to find myself sniveling into the phone, but I was consumed with a sense of guilt at having deceived Stone. "I'm so sorry. Please forgive me. I really didn't mean to worry you."

"It's okay, honey. I'm sure I would have balked because I can't help but worry about you, but the main thing is that you're all right. When Crystal came and told me Rosalinda was up in the room with you, I rushed right up there and was terrified to find you missing. Rosalinda claimed to have no idea where you'd gone, but she was well on her way to getting inebriated, and I don't trust her anyway. I called your cell phone and got your voice mail. I left a message but you never returned my call."

"Oh, I'm sorry. I forgot to turn it on until I had to call for a wrecker," I said.

"A wrecker? Oh, no! What happened? Have you been in an accident?"

"No, no. It's nothing like that. The Jeep is just stuck in a ditch. Doug's Towing will soon be here to pull me out, and then I'll head straight to the Alexandria Inn. I'll tell you all about everything then. Okay?"

Stone was understandably annoyed with me when I returned early in the afternoon, but his sense of relief overwhelmed his anger. Still, I knew his patience had to be wearing pretty thin with my recent impulsive antics. He listened patiently as I reiterated my conversations with Rosalinda and then her half-brother Peter Randall. I told him Detective Johnston had stopped and visited with me when he spotted my Jeep in the ditch, and then I told him about my visit to the Farm and Ranch Supply store. As always, Stone listened intently as I spoke, and when I finished, he told me I had a message to call Wendy at her home. Harry Turner had told him he wanted to talk to me, too, when I had some free time.

We were sitting at the counter in the kitchen, drinking coffee and scanning through the *Rockdale Gazette,* which Stone had just retrieved from the front yard. It was several hours late in being delivered, which didn't come as any surprise to me. I knew the carrier, Howie Clamm, had been towed out of a ditch earlier, too.

Stone read the front-page article aloud. It concerned the investigation into Prescott's murder and the arrest of Peter Randall as the prime suspect, so it was conceivable Stacey Shryock could have read about Peter's arrest, after all. As Stone held the paper up to read the front page, I noticed a small headline on the back of the paper. It read *Indian Rights Committee Snuffs*

Development Plan.

A few minutes later, I would read the entire article and realize the property in question was the land selected as the site of the new shopping center downtown. It was the property Horatio had bought out from under Robert Fischer and was in preparation of selling to a developer for six and a half million dollars. Only now, during the surveying stage, in the middle of the acreage, an ancient Indian burial plot had been discovered and the project had been stalled. It contained the remains of six long-dead Native Americans from the Pottawatomie tribe. For now, at least, no development would be allowed to take place on what was considered sacred land. It now appeared that Robert Fischer was fortunate he hadn't invested in this particular property, which was suddenly worth less than half what Horatio had paid for it years ago.

CHAPTER SEVENTEEN

I finished reading the newspaper and made myself a peanut butter and jelly sandwich. I'd missed lunch at the inn, and my stomach was growling. I made a sandwich for Stone, too, because he'd eaten early and was hungry again. I liked the fact that, like me, Stone carried around a few extra pounds. It made him cuddlier and made me feel less chubby. It also lent him a reliable air, which I found reassuring.

Crystal was scouring counters in the kitchen and offered to make the sandwiches for us, but I declined her offer with a wave of my hand. She was cleaning up after the lunch she'd just served to our Historical Society guests. She had enough on her plate without waiting on us hand and foot. In one fluid motion, Crystal tossed the soiled washrag in the sink and opened the dishwasher, which was full of still steaming clean dishes. She was placing a stack of plates in the cabinet before I could even open my mouth to speak.

"It'll only take me a minute, sweetie," I said. "But thanks for the offer anyway. After you finish unloading the dishwasher, why don't you take a much-deserved coffee break yourself?"

"I might," she said. "I've already had too much coffee today, but I could use a glass of iced tea."

"Take a break now if you'd like, Crystal," Stone said. "The dishes can wait."

The kitchen phone rang as he spoke, and he crossed the room to answer it. I could tell it was Detective Johnston on the other end. When Stone hung up, he turned to me with a grin and a thumbs-up gesture.

"Detective Johnston asked me to tell you that you were correct," Stone said. "After he spoke to Sergeant O'Brien about your idea, the sergeant sent him over to Peter Randall's house to take a Polaroid photo of Peter with his glasses on and without the hairpiece. Randall had forgotten he hadn't worn the toupee or his contacts to the theatre. Wyatt took the new photo over to the usher's house and the young kid recognized Peter immediately as the man he woke in the theatre Sunday night. The kid said Mr. Randall fell asleep during the previews of coming attractions, before the featured movie even began. He admitted he hadn't recognized the man in the first photo he'd been shown because it was a photo taken of Mr. Randall at work, wearing his toupee, contacts, and a formal suit. It looked like a totally different person."

"I had a gut feeling that's what had happened," I said.

"Your intuition paid off. The lady who sold the movie ticket to Mr. Randall also recognized him in the new photo and stated she saw him leave the theatre after the show and walk across the street to his house. She could see him open his front door from her ticket booth. She said all his lights went out shortly afterwards, as if he'd gone straight to bed. The house remained dark until she left the theatre at quitting time."

"So his story's been validated?"

"Yes. The charges against him have been dropped, and because Peter Randall was the only suspect they'd come up with, the Rockdale Police Department has decided to turn the case over to the county homicide division. The county has a larger staff and more experience dealing with this kind of thing."

"What a relief!" I said. "On both counts, I might add."

"Horatio's daughter Veronica must have thought so, too. Wyatt said she decided not to retain her own P.I. once she heard the county homicide division was taking over the case. Veronica felt they were better equipped to handle the investigation, I'm sure."

"It stands to reason they would be," I agreed. "Rockdale's not a very big town and doesn't have a very extensive police force. I don't think it'd be wise to have the entire force tied up with one homicide case anyway, even as rare as homicide is for this town. Rockdale's not exactly a hotbed of crime, but things are always going on that need the attention of police officers."

"You're probably right," Stone said. "And also, Wyatt told me Veronica had recently divorced her Mormon husband, which caused quite a stir. Apparently her husband was abusive. Broke her jaw the last time he pounded on her. Veronica's in town for her father's funeral, and Wyatt is going to escort her to the services. He's picking her up at the airport this afternoon. He's kind of excited and surprised she'd lower herself to accept his help. He told me he had a crush on her when he was younger, but she'd had no interest in him whatsoever. I told him to remember people can change over the years, for better or worse."

I nodded. "That'd be nice if they hit it off. Wyatt is an attractive man, and he seems like the type who'd be happier with a wife and family. He definitely needs a wife who likes to cook. Speaking of family, Rosalinda will be happy to hear the news about her brother. I think I'll go tell her right now," I said.

"You'll probably find Rosalinda's a bit tipsy." Stone chuckled and gave me a wink. "She's been in the parlor with Cornelius for a couple of hours. The two of them seem to be getting pretty tight—in more ways than one."

"She's with the handsome devil himself?"

"Huh?"

I left him with a puzzled look on his face and went to tell Rosalinda the good news about Peter. After speaking with

Rosalinda, I'd search for Harry Turner.

As I suspected, Rosalinda was ecstatic the police had dropped charges on Peter, or at least she was ecstatic once she remembered who Peter was and why he'd been arrested in the first place. I found her giggling like a schoolgirl in response to something Cornelius had just said as they frolicked playfully on the loveseat near the fireplace. "Wank woo, Wexie," Rosalinda said, after I explained the good news.

"Have you seen Harry Turner recently?" I asked Cornelius. I could see that conversing with Rosalinda was just a waste of my time.

"No, sorry," he said. "He's may be reading in the library with Alma or in his room packing his suitcase. We're all planning to leave after lunch tomorrow. We decided to give the streets a chance to dry off before we headed out. They could still be a bit slick in the morning."

It seemed as if none of the Historical Society guests were in a hurry to leave the Alexandria Inn. They apparently were becoming quite accustomed to being waited on and now didn't want to return to their mundane everyday lives, lives that required them to be more self-reliant. I'd heard both Ernestine Fischer and Harry Turner tell Crystal to call them if she ever needed a job because they would be delighted to have her work for them as a housekeeper in their private homes. She had smiled sweetly and promised she'd keep their offers in mind.

At least there was a light at the end of our long, dark tunnel, I thought, as I went in search of Harry Turner in the library. We could surely tolerate these folks for one more day. Couldn't we?

Alma was in the library by herself, with a book titled *Death March* on the desk in front of her. The book was opened to a page with a drawing depicting one of the gas chambers employed by Adolf Hitler. I would have thought she could find something a little less depressing than gas chambers to read about, even though she didn't actually seem to be reading the book, but rather using it to hide behind.

"How was lunch, Alma?"

"It was fine, thank you," she said. I nodded, even though I knew she hadn't eaten anything. Crystal had told me neither Boris Dack nor the Turners had shown up for lunch. "It was just fine," Alma said again from behind the book.

She was oddly distracted, as if her mind were miles away from the book she had propped up in front of her. I doubt she'd have even noticed if the book were upside down. Alma appeared ill at ease and wouldn't look me in the eye. She was fidgeting in her chair, and her skin looked flushed and clammy. Something had definitely happened to upset her. Her eyes were darting all over the place, never resting more than a second or two on any object.

"Are you all right, Mrs. Turner?"

"Yes, of course. I'm fine. Why wouldn't I be?"

"You just seem a little agitated today, a bit nervous and edgy."

"Well, I may be a bit edgy. Who wouldn't be, under the circumstances? The murder, and all that's happened since, has been a little unnerving for all of us," Alma said. "You surely are a bit edgy yourself with what you've been through."

"You're right. We're all a bit on edge, myself included. I need to get home to my little place in Shawnee for a break from all the excitement. Are you looking forward to going home tomorrow? I hear everyone is planning to leave the inn after lunch," I said.

"Oh, really? I hadn't heard that. But yes, I suppose I'm looking forward to going home tomorrow, even though some things will never be the same again. Once I'm home, that is. Staying here the last few days has been a very distressing experience for me. Uh, well, you know, because of the appalling murder of Mr. Prescott, naturally."

"Yes, of course. Something like a murder does tend to put a damper on things, doesn't it?"

Alma had not seemed to be terribly distressed by the "appalling murder" of Horatio Prescott, but she did seemed suddenly distressed about something. I wondered what she meant by her remark "things will never be the same" once she'd returned home. I wanted to ask her to explain her comment but knew it'd be a waste of time. She'd never air her dirty laundry—she'd made that clear before—so I changed the subject.

"Can I get you anything from the kitchen? I'm going there after I take care of a few other matters."

"A cup of hot tea does sound good. Jasmine to calm my nerves, I think, and a couple of those wonderful oatmeal cookies that Crystal was baking earlier would be much appreciated. When you have the time. For some reason, lunch didn't appease my appetite." I wanted to ask if failing to show up to eat any of it had anything to do with her hunger not being appeased.

"No problem, Mrs. Turner. Stay here so I don't have to track you down, and I'll be back in a few minutes." I wanted to keep her waiting in the library while I tracked down her husband for a one-on-one discussion. I hoped he was still in his room packing his suitcase. I hurried out of the library.

As I left, Alma Turner was staring out the window, over the top of the opened book about the Nazi dictator. I wondered what had happened to make her so distraught.

Harry was in his room, but he wasn't packing his suitcase as Cornelius had suggested. He was pacing anxiously, as keyed-up as his wife had been. I could hear his footfalls from outside his room. I tapped on his door, and he opened it quickly as if he'd been waiting impatiently for someone to knock.

"Oh, good. I was hoping it was you, Lexie," he said, reaching for my elbow, pulling me in his room. "You aren't going to believe what happened this morning, just before lunch." Harry said, in an excited tone. I would have been concerned if not for the grin stretching across his face.

"I just spoke to Alma in the library, Harry. She seemed quite anxious, as if something was really worrying her. Is everything all right?"

"For me, yes, but not for her. Alma has every reason to be anxious and worried," he said. There was a glint in his eye that almost frightened me. He pulled the chair away from the small desk in his room and motioned for me to sit down. "Have a seat and let me tell you what happened when I attempted to follow your advice and speak to Boris Dack about the photo in Horatio's safe."

"The photo—"

"The one of me in Alma's negligee, of course." Harry's face flushed a light shade of pink as he made the clarification. I hadn't actually forgotten which photo was involved. That was a tough image to get out of one's mind.

"Oh, so you spoke to Boris about the photo today?" I asked.

"No, but I don't think the photo is going to be an issue any longer. I'd bet my bottom dollar the blackmailing is a thing of the past at this point."

"Oh, really? What happened? Tell me all about it." I was almost as excited as Harry now—and more than a little relieved that my advice hadn't backfired in his face.

"Well, I wanted to talk to him at the first opportunity but didn't want to do so in Alma's presence. This morning, right after breakfast, Alma told me she had the beginning of a headache forming behind her forehead. I suggested she take one of her headache pills and go back to bed for a while. She vetoed my idea, saying she'd only be awakened by someone knocking on the door, which could cause her headache to worsen. I knew Boris was up in his room, and I wanted to seize the opportunity to speak to him about the photo, so I promised Alma she wouldn't be bothered. I told her I'd hang the 'Do Not Disturb' placard from the doorknob and make sure everyone knew she was resting, nursing one of her headaches, and didn't want to be disturbed."

"But, she's in the library now, and never mentioned a head—"

"She never had a headache, my dear," Harry cut in.

"But you said—"

"Alma lied to me about having a headache, I'm certain, just to make sure I didn't come up here looking for her."

"But why?"

"After Alma came upstairs, presumably to our room to rest, I went to Boris's door with the intention of discussing the photograph with him. I heard laughter in his room, so I put my ear up against the door. It was barely discernable, but it was unmistakably Alma's laugh. Lord knows, I'd recognize that hideous sound anywhere."

"Alma was in Boris's room?" I couldn't hide my amazement, or my confusion.

"Yes, I was shocked, too," Harry said. "And she was in a very compromising position when I slipped a credit card into the lock on his door and freed it open. When I burst into the room, they both were butt naked, cavorting in the middle of his bed, and the look on their faces was absolutely priceless."

"Oh my God! I can't imagine—"

"And guess what? I will have a photo of those expressions, to keep as a souvenir of this week here at the Alexandria Inn, just as soon as I take this disposable camera to be developed," Harry said, as he picked up a yellow, red, and black cardboard camera off his dresser. He held it up as it were a golden Oscar he'd just been awarded at the Academy Awards show.

"You didn't!" I was laughing out loud.

"I most certainly did. One good blackmail-quality photo deserves another, don't you think? I have a close friend who owns a one-hour photo lab who'll be happy to print this for me this afternoon, despite the content of the photo. I just got off the phone with him."

"How did you happen to have the camera with you?"

"Alma had it in her overnight bag. She'd brought it with her to snap photos at the inauguration ceremony, which was naturally canceled when Prescott was killed. I'd placed it in the pocket of my cardigan earlier with the intention of taking pictures of the large snowdrift beside the carport. I never did go out and take those pictures, but the camera was still in my pocket. When I heard Alma laughing inside Boris's room, I instinctively took the camera out and warmed up the flash. I snapped a photo the second I opened the door and saw them exposed on the bed."

I could scarcely contain my amusement at the thought of Harry snapping a photo of the pair on Boris's bed or my revulsion at the image that slowly formed in my mind, like a Polaroid snapshot gradually coming into focus.

"What happened next?" I asked Harry.

"Alma shrieked, grabbed her clothes, and ran across the hall to lock herself in our room while she dressed. Boris grabbed the bedspread to wrap around his flaccid naked body. Egad, talk about hideous!"

"I can well imagine." I tried not to even think about it or picture the image on that photograph.

"He seemed afraid; as if he feared I'd pull out a gun and shoot him. Maybe Boris thought I was the person who killed his partner. I don't really know what went through his mind. He was uttering something like, 'It's not what you think.' Of course,

I knew it was exactly what I thought, but I didn't really care."

"What'd you say to him?"

"I merely asked him if he'd like to make an even exchange. My photo of him with my wife for Horatio's photo of me in her clothes. He obviously knew all about the photo and the monthly payments I'd been making to keep the photo out of sight because he readily agreed to the deal. He promised to extract the photo from the company safe this evening. He said he had an important meeting at six tonight—"

"Uh-huh," I said with a knowing nod.

"—but he'd stop by his office to get the photo on the way to the meeting. He'd gladly trade photos with me tomorrow morning, before breakfast. Which reminds me, Lexie. Can I borrow your Jeep for about an hour? My Mercedes may not do well in this snow, and I'd like to take this camera over to my friend's place today. Jack lives in an apartment above his photo shop, and since there's only one photo on the roll, it shouldn't take too long."

"Why does the film even need to be developed?" I asked.

"It doesn't. I could just give the whole camera to Boris in exchange for the photo of me in the negligee, but I'd kind of like to have the negative to put in my lock box. Just in case I ever need it, if you know what I mean. I'll also have Jack print me an extra copy of the photo, just in case Boris thinks to demand the negative, too."

"Yes, I completely understand your need to take precautions. I wouldn't trust Boris Dack any further than Robert Fischer can throw a water buffalo. Can you leave right away? I've already promised to loan my Jeep to Boris this evening, to get to the meeting he mentioned to you, and he said he'd like to leave here by five."

Harry checked his watch, nodded, and said, "Sure. It's about two now, so I'd have it back by three, or three-thirty at the latest. I promise to be back no later than four, even if it means picking up the copies of the photo in the morning."

"Okay, I'll get the keys for you. I'm delighted it worked out so well, Harry, but sorry about the circumstances regarding Alma's affair with Mr. Dack." It had not escaped me that Harry hadn't showed much remorse about the fact his wife had been cheating on him, committing adultery with the contemptible Boris Dack, of all people. If anything, he seemed delighted, acting as if things couldn't have turned out any better for him.

"Oh, don't feel badly about that aspect of it," he said. "Any love I'd felt for Alma had gone by the wayside a long time ago. It didn't bother me in the least the two of them were having an affair, other than the fact I was being played for a fool. I'm just glad Boris wasn't aware of the tenuous relationship I had with my wife, or I might have lost my leverage in this deal. I've been unhappy with Alma for many years, but I think that's all about to change. I spoke with her a few minutes ago in the library, right before you did, in fact. She was mortified beyond belief, and hiding behind some large, boring tome about Hitler. She was afraid of what I might do or say and couldn't bring herself to look me in the eye."

"Go on," I said, encouraging him.

"She agreed to file for a divorce—a quiet, uncontested divorce. We would split our assets equally and go our separate ways. The assets are all essentially hers, but she's agreed to give up half of them as her end of the deal. For my end of the deal, I promised to never mention what I observed this morning. I knew the last thing Alma would want is the rumor going around about her having an affair with Boris Dack. It wouldn't fare well with her quilting club buddies."

As I listened to Harry Turner, it occurred to me he was now blackmailing his wife in much the same manner as Horatio had blackmailed him all those years. Does one bad turn really deserve another? I didn't really think so. But despite it all, I couldn't help feeling pleased about the way things had turned out for Harry.

I told him I was happy to know the defamatory photo would no longer be an issue for him and expressed condolences on the dissolution of his marriage, all in one breath. He thanked me once again for giving him the push he needed to confront Boris about the photo in the first place. "Without your encouragement, my dear, things could have gone on in the same intolerable fashion as before. I'd have stayed with Alma, hating every minute I spent with her. And I'd have continued to pay Boris to keep my shameful secret from the rest of the world, while he and my wife were keeping their shameful secret from me."

Yes, that was it! Harry had just, in one sentence, explained to me why I felt pleased with myself for helping Harry find an answer to his dilemma. What Harry had done wasn't right, but it wasn't quite as despicable as what others had done to him. Wasn't that some kind of twisted version of the Golden Rule? I wondered.

I congratulated Harry once more before leaving to take tea and cookies to Alma in the library and then find Stone. I was anxious to relate this latest development to him. I just prayed the conjured-up vision of Alma Turner "cavorting butt-naked" with Boris Dack wasn't something that would linger in my mind for very long.

CHAPTER EIGHTEEN

"Hey there, Mom!" I heard when I picked up the ringing phone as I stepped into the kitchen.

"Hi, Wendy."

I glanced out the window over the sink and saw Stone in the backyard. He was talking to Otto Poffenbarger. It was the first time I'd ever seen Otto without his spouse. Always before he'd been following in Patty's wake, like a puppy waiting for her to hand him a bone to chew on. I turned my attention back to Wendy.

"Anything new?" she asked. "Stone called and told me you were pushed down the staircase last night. Were you injured? I couldn't believe what he was saying. Any ideas about who might have shoved you? Didn't anybody see anything? Didn't you get a glimpse of the culprit yourself? Are you feeling okay today? Why are you still intermingling with any of them, anyway? Didn't Stone tell you to back off on your personal investigation? Didn't he say the success of the inn was not worth your getting injured, or worse? How could you even think about—?"

"Yes, Wendy, I'm fine." As usual, Wendy was firing questions at me like a pitching machine throwing balls at warp speed to a batter. I selected the most innocuous question to answer and hoped it would satisfy her. "Just ended up with a few bumps and bruises, that's all."

"I'll certainly be relieved when all those damn Historical Society people leave the inn. This is really starting to scare me.

Somebody there is obviously determined to harm you and, given enough time and opportunities, they will!"

"It does seem as if someone wants me out of the way, doesn't it?" I wanted to derail the conversation away from the current subject. Wendy had an annoying propensity to treat me as if I had the intelligence of a barnacle. Maybe it was true I hadn't exhibited much common sense recently, but it didn't mean I wanted to be lectured about it by my own daughter. She didn't seem to think I could survive without a lot of help and advice, mainly from her. I changed the subject before she could get up on the soapbox I knew she was steering toward. "So what's new with you?"

"I just got home from work and thought I'd call to check on you and tell you what I learned regarding the Prescott homicide."

"Oh? What'd you learn?" The distraction ploy had worked, veering Wendy away from discussing her mother and her mother's erratic and irrational behavior.

"The county homicide investigators came and spoke with Nate and me today. They discovered the only place in the entire region selling tansy oil is the Dunsten Drug Store in St. Joseph."

Dunsten Drug Store. Why did the name sound so familiar? I knew I'd heard of it before, but I couldn't remember where or when. "So the tansy oil was purchased there?" I asked my daughter.

"No," Wendy said. "Mr. Dunsten checked himself but found no record of having sold any tansy oil in months. Dunsten Drug is a small, old-fashioned, family-owned drug store and has been known to carry a lot of unusual, off-the-wall items in their inventory. It's the place to look if you can't find something anywhere else, and that's probably what's kept them in business for so many years."

"That'd be a good thing to remember. So it would appear the tansy oil was purchased outside of the Kansas City area?"

"That's the assumption at this point."

"Everything else okay at home? I feel like I haven't been there in weeks."

"Everything's fine. And Andy called last night with some great news. He's very seriously considering selling out in Myrtle Beach and moving back to this area. Andy's always wanted to own a farm, and he found some acreage just west of Rockdale listed in a classified ad on the Internet. The property has an old farmhouse on it, a nice barn, and several out buildings. It also comes with a John Deere tractor, a rooster and chickens, a handful of hogs, a goat, and seventy-three head of Black Angus. It's exactly what he's been dreaming about and at a price he thinks he can swing. I promised Andy I'd run by the property and take some digital photos to e-mail to him."

"Oh, Wendy, that's great news. But can he make a living at farming?"

"He's not sure, but he wants to try, and I promised I'd help him any way I can," Wendy said. "He's planning to keep his five-passenger Cessna so he can still take on charter flights out of the industrial airport here."

"Stone will be so pleased to hear the news. There's nothing he'd like more than to see his favorite nephew relocate to this area. That's really the only reservation Stone had about leaving Myrtle Beach."

"There's nothing I'd like more, either, Mom, than to have Andy move back here like Stone did. Andy's such a great guy, just like his uncle."

"I know. He's so much like Stone it's uncanny. Listen, Wendy, I need to get off the phone. Speaking of Stone, I see him visiting with Mr. Poffenbarger in the backyard, and I'd like to go out and talk to them."

"Mom," Wendy said, dragging the three-letter word out like it had five syllables. "Can't you just drop it? How do you know Mr. Poffenbarger's not the one who shoved you down the stairs? Who's to say he didn't shoot Mr. Prescott?"

"Oh, I really don't think Otto would—"

"Didn't you say he and Prescott were both writing books about the same subject? Isn't there bound to be a lot of competition between them to get their own book published first?"

"Yes, of course, dear. But I'll be perfectly safe. Stone will be here with me. Try not to worry so much. It's not good for your health to be under so much stress," I cautioned. I sighed as I hung up the phone and went out the back door of the kitchen to speak to Stone and Otto.

"Hi, hon."

"Hello, Ms. Starr."

The two men, standing over an empty raised flowerbed, greeted me in unison. The soil had been tilled in preparation for planting flowers after the frost-free date had passed. Otto gestured toward the flowerbed as he spoke.

"I was just giving Stone some tips on how to make the soil more fertile. Fertile soil will help your flowers grow and stay healthy."

"Oh? I'd like to discuss it with you sometime, too. I have some landscaping ideas I'm anxious to experiment with this spring," I said. It was then I noticed a large manuscript lying on one of the patio tables to the left of the two gentlemen. Stone caught my surprised expression.

"I just brought it out to show to Otto," he said. He shot me a meaningful look. "It's the book Mr. Prescott had been working on. I was telling Otto how Mr. Prescott's manuscript had been found in Otto's suitcase, and he's assured me he has absolutely no idea how it got there. He's concerned someone was attempting to frame him by planting it there. I agree it's possible."

"It sure looks like it, doesn't it?" I picked up the stack of loose pages, probably three or four hundred in all, and flipped through them.

With a look of discomfort, Otto said, "Stone allowed me to scan through the first couple of chapters. I was eager to get a sense of Horatio's writing style, just out of curiosity, of course. I have to admit, it's very good—much better than mine. It deserves to be published, and my book pales in comparison, I'm afraid. For my book to have any prayer of being published, I'd have to completely revise it. I'd need to add humor and make it a lot less dry and more interesting. And frankly, I don't believe I have the capacity, the talent, or the patience to do it."

"So what are you saying, Otto?" I asked.

"I'm going to put my manuscript on the shelf for now and offer to help Horatio's daughter, Veronica, get her father's book published. He put a lot of effort into it, and even if his book were published posthumously, it'd be better than it not being published at all. His expertise really shines through in his writing, and this how-to book would be quite an asset to people attempting to restore historic homes a proper and accurate way. I'm man enough to admit my book couldn't hold a candle to his. It's a shame he won't be around to enjoy his success with it."

"Otto, I think that's a wonderful idea," I said. Stone nodded his agreement. I set the manuscript back on the table and continued, "It says a lot about your character and integrity. And I'm sure your writing is not as bad as you make it sound."

"Well, thanks, but I'm just doing what anyone with an ounce of common sense would do," Otto said. "Now I should go upstairs and leave you two alone. Stone, I trust you'll see this manuscript is turned over to the authorities?"

"Yes, of course," Stone said.

We watched Otto Poffenbarger walk up to the back deck and then open the door into the parlor. Once he was out of view I turned to Stone. "That's thoughtful of him. Isn't it? Otto seems different to me. Does he to you?"

"Uh-huh," Stone agreed. "Something clicked in him last night after Patty choked on the chicken bone at the supper table. It was like the proverbial straw breaking the camel's back. Before you came out here he told me he and Patty had engaged in an argument after supper, a battle of wills he called it. Otto told her he couldn't tolerate the situation any longer and threatened to file for divorce. By the time the dust settled, Patty had agreed to stop treating Otto as a subordinate and also to make a formidable effort to lose weight."

"That will be the day."

"Well, it won't be easy for her, but she's considering gastric bypass surgery, like Al Roker on the *Today Show* had done. And Crystal told me Patty turned down doughnuts with her coffee this morning and requested just grapefruit for breakfast and a small salad for lunch. That's certainly a good start."

"I'll say! Good for her! I'm proud of her. We'll have to encourage Patty and offer whatever support we can. If she doesn't do something drastic soon, her heart could give out from having to work too hard. Her arteries have to be pretty clogged too, I'd imagine."

"Otto did tell me Patty's cholesterol level was dangerously high. She's a borderline diabetic and has high blood pressure, too. And she really does have a thyroid condition, but one little iodine tablet a day controls it and keeps it at a normal level. Being grossly obese only exacerbates all of her medical problems, Otto said. Anyway, I hope Patty's willpower holds out, and that everything works out for them."

"Yeah, me too," I agreed.

"And how are you doing, Lexie? Feel okay?"

"I feel pretty good, actually. And I just talked to Wendy on the phone before I came out here."

"What'd she have to say?" Stone asked.

"She had some great news about Andy, for one thing. But let's go inside and get a cup of coffee. It's cold out here. We can talk in the kitchen. I have an interesting story to tell you about Boris Dack and the Turners, too."

Placing one arm around my shoulder, Stone picked up Horatio's manuscript with the other. "I'm sure you do. Oh, and don't worry," he said. "I didn't tell Otto who discovered the manuscript in his luggage."

I nodded in relief as Stone guided me into the inn. As we passed through the parlor we saw Robert Fischer lay the newspaper on the coffee table. We then overheard him say to his wife Ernestine, "You know, I've always said things happen for a reason, haven't I? Now we finally know why our attempt to buy the property downtown never came to fruition. Thank God for unanswered prayers."

The last thing we heard as we walked through the kitchen door was Ernestine's gleeful laughter. "I guess Bert and Ernie got the last laugh after all, didn't they?" she said.

CHAPTER NINETEEN

Harry Turner returned with my Jeep at about ten minutes before four. He pulled me aside to show me the photo he'd snapped of his wife in a compromising position with Boris Dack. Boris's hairy, naked butt, which was as chalky white as the snow outside, filled most of the photo—and it wasn't a pretty sight. Both he and Alma's faces were turned toward the camera. The looks on their faces indicated pure terror and shock. Harry's photograph left no doubt as to the situation or the participants. I could feel my last sip of coffee rising back up to my throat. Geez, there was five minutes of my life I'd never get back.

I gave Harry a faint smile and a thumbs-up as I reached for my car keys. He thanked me for lending him my vehicle and again for encouraging him to approach Boris about the blackmail extortion he'd been subjected to for years.

I told Harry that although Mr. Dack had already had a bad day, there was a good chance it was going to get much, much worse before it was over. Not wanting to take a chance word of the sting operation could leak out, I promised Harry I'd give him a thorough explanation the following day. He was intrigued and hardly able to contain his curiosity.

"How exciting," he said. "Now I'll be like a kid waiting impatiently for Santa Claus to come down the chimney on Christmas Eve. This has been a most eventful few days."

I left Harry, took the keys to my Jeep, and went straight to Boris Dack's room. Boris appeared even more agitated than

Alma had when I'd spoken to her earlier in the library. He was almost pathetic as he reached out with a trembling hand for the keys. He mumbled a curt, "Thanks," and nearly shut his door in my face. I felt nothing but disdain for this rude, repulsive man. If I weren't in the process of setting him up, I wouldn't have lent him my car.

I was as giddy in anticipation as Harry Turner was. I could hardly wait to hear what transpired at Boris Dack's six o'clock meeting with Pablo Pikstone, Shorty, four endangered kakapo parrots—and an uninvited SWAT team.

As expected, everyone but Boris Dack appeared for supper. Crystal and I served a rack of lamb with new potatoes and asparagus. Crystal had even baked a red velvet cake for dessert. I noticed Alma staring down at her plate, refusing to make eye contact with anyone. She ate her meal systematically, like a programmed robot, and excused herself from the table before dessert was served.

Patty Poffenbarger spoke sparingly and merely played with her food, rearranging it on her plate to appear as if she'd eaten the bulk of it, when actually she'd only taken about a half dozen small bites. She ate all of her tossed salad, but declined a serving of the red velvet cake, although she stared at Otto's plate the entire time he ate his dessert. She was nearly salivating as she asked him if Crystal's cake was as good as the red velvet cake she often made.

Otto judiciously told Patty that both recipes were delicious. Otto was exhibiting a much more assertive personality than anyone could have anticipated. This new attitude must have been hidden deep within him for all the years he'd allowed his wife to control his every move. He even seemed surprised at himself as he then told a slightly off-color joke. Patty laughed louder than anyone else at the table did. The punch line made no sense to me, so she was apparently trying to placate her husband.

Harry laughed politely at Otto's pathetic attempt at humor. Harry was in high spirits. He winked at me across the table. I noticed he sat two chairs down from Alma and didn't even blink when she left the table early. He was as emotionally detached from Alma as he could be. It was not love that had kept them together all these years but a fear of embarrassment, I concluded.

Cornelius was seated next to Rosalinda Swift. He held her chair for her as she sat down at the table. Rosalinda, for once, appeared to be completely sober. She was clearly wallowing in Cornelius's attention.

Robert and Ernestine Fischer were also buoyant, as if a heavy weight had been lifted off their shoulders. Bert and Ernie were thanking their lucky stars that Horatio Prescott had screwed them out of a land deal years ago and saved them from a financial catastrophe.

All in all, it was a vastly transformed group that sat down for their last supper at Alexandria Inn. The death of Horatio Prescott III had set in motion a chain of events precipitating a metamorphosis within the Historical Society. And more life-altering events were probable, I realized, as I looked at my watch and saw it was half past six. Boris might already be in custody, I realized with a start. What I wouldn't give to be a mouse at that little get-together.

It was hard to believe how much had changed in a matter of a few days. And yet, there was probably an undetected killer among the group sitting around the supper table. I was no closer to determining which of them was responsible for the murder of Prescott and the attempts on my life than I had been early Monday morning. In that respect, absolutely nothing had changed.

CHAPTER TWENTY

It was late, a quarter to eleven, when Wyatt Johnston knocked on the door leading into the inn's kitchen. All the guests had retired to their rooms for the night, and Stone and I were visiting in the kitchen over glasses of milk and a couple of Crystal's oatmeal cookies. Stone looked through the peephole before opening the door.

Wyatt removed his snow-encrusted boots, shrugged off his jacket, and sat down at the table. "I noticed your kitchen light was the only one burning in the house or I'd have gone to the front door. I was hoping it was you two in the kitchen."

I poured the detective a glass of milk and placed a plate full of cookies before him. He popped an entire cookie in his mouth and washed it down with a huge gulp of milk. Still holding the pitcher in my right hand, I refilled his glass and put the rest of the milk on the table in front of him. This big, burly cop was a bottomless pit, yet there didn't seem to be an ounce of fat on his frame.

After he inhaled another cookie, he said, "Umm, very tasty. That gal you hired is an awesome cook, isn't she?"

"Uh-huh, Crystal's a genius in the kitchen. We lucked out with her," Stone said.

"You sure did! Well, I wanted to stop by and let you know the sting operation at the Pikstone compound went down perfectly. Thanks to you, Ms. Starr, the four kakapos are already on their way back home to New Zealand, and all of them seem to be healthy and hardy."

"What happened? Tell us all about it," I said, excitement in my voice.

"As expected, Boris stopped by his office on Executive Drive. The FBI agents waited a block up the street while he was inside for about ten minutes. Then they followed him out to Pablo's place off I-70. They parked their cars a couple of blocks away and walked the rest of the way, positioning themselves out of sight around the compound. At almost six o'clock, a man named Mortimer Sharp, who has a rap sheet a mile long and stands about six and a half feet tall or better, drove up to the Pikstone property in a Land Rover."

"Shorty?" I asked. Mortimer Sharp was the name I'd come up with in my phone number crosscheck on the computer.

"Yeah, that's what Boris called him. Pablo Pikstone had walked out earlier when Boris arrived, and they both greeted the tall guy, who had a cage in the back of the Land Rover with the four parrots in it. Odd-looking critters. Looked like green owls to me. Smelled funny, too. But anyway, the FBI team converged on Boris, Shorty, and Pablo, and Boris pulled out a gun."

"Thirty-two caliber?" Stone asked.

"Nah, it was a forty-five."

"A forty-five?"

"Yeah, it was a Kimber Ultra Carry, a handgun that is fairly easy to conceal," Wyatt said around a mouthful of oatmeal cookie. "But Boris didn't fire it, thank goodness. He quickly realized he was outgunned when Sergeant O'Brien, six FBI agents, and I all drew down on him at the same time. He threw aside his gun and surrendered. Mortimer Sharp turned out to not be very sharp at all. The fool started to make a run for it, but when I fired a shot in his vicinity, 'Shorty' thought better of the idea and dropped down to the ground with his hands clasped behind his head."

"And Pablo Pikstone?" Stone asked.

"He just shook his head in disgust, as though admonishing himself for dealing with such inept characters as Boris and Shorty, and turned around quietly to be cuffed. The whole take-down took less than two minutes. Smooth as silk, no shots fired."

"Think Boris will do some time?" I asked.

"Yes, I'm pretty sure he will. I'm not sure how much he'll get for the parrot-napping caper, but there's been an ongoing undercover investigation of his business practices, and it looks like he'll be indicted on a long list of charges including racketeering, extortion, embezzlement, money-laundering and insurance fraud. They even have proof he was soliciting donations for a phony charity claiming to aid children with cancer and young burn victims. The guy's a class act, let me tell you."

"That's outrageous! I hope the jerk never sees daylight again," I said angrily. "Even life in prison would be too good for the likes of him. I can't imagine anyone using critically sick children as a means of extorting money out of people."

"Neither can I, and at his age, I really wouldn't be too surprised to see him live out the rest of his life in prison." Wyatt snagged another cookie, popped it into his mouth, swallowing it like a starving Rottweiler might swallow a chunk of raw meat, and then continued speaking.

"A representative employed by New Zealand's DOC was on hand to take over custody of the birds. He will accompany and care for the kakapos. He and the parrots are already en route back to Codfish Island, the island they were waiting to be transferred to," Detective Johnston explained. "By the way, Lexie, I heard the rep say the DOC was discussing some form of reward to be presented to you for your courage and your quick thinking. It allowed them to apprehend those scumbags and save the kakapos. The reward would be something in the neighborhood of ten thousand dollars, he said. They feel if it weren't for you and your actions, they might have never located the abducted kakapos, and every one of the eighty-six remaining parrots is critical to their recovery program. They are very grateful and very relieved."

"Oh, gosh," I said, embarrassed by the praise. I hadn't expected or envisioned a reward, especially not of that magnitude. My only concern had been for the parrots and the future of the endangered species. "That's really not necessary. I didn't do it for a monetary reward."

"I know, and they know you didn't," Wyatt said. "But I still think the reward is well-deserved. Most people would've hesitated to get involved."

"Wyatt's right," Stone agreed. "And what you ultimately decide to do about it is obviously up to you. I'll back whatever decision you make. I have to hand it to you, though. It took a lot of guts on your part, and I'm proud of you, even though it probably did take ten years off my life." Stone gave me an affectionate hug.

"Thank you, Stone. That means a lot to me," I said. "But I just did what any responsible citizen would have done. You know, ten thousand dollars could go a long way in the kakapo recovery efforts. If they offer me a reward, I'm going to accept it because I don't want to offend them. But then I'm going to donate the ten thousand dollars back to the recovery program and ask if there's some way I can volunteer my efforts in soliciting other donations on their behalf."

Stone gazed at me with an expression of awe. "Ah, my dear, I wholeheartedly agree with your decision. You're one-in-a-million. Do you know that?" he said softly. "Not many people would be so thoughtful and unselfish. I'm certainly lucky you found me."

"I agree with Stone," Wyatt said. "That's very generous of

you. And speaking of lucky, I spent the afternoon with Veronica, and she's agreed to go on a date with me after her father's wake and funeral are behind her. She's changed a lot since high school. She's mellowed, become a lot more humble and a lot less high strung. I guess I've changed, too. In my younger days, I was too shy to ask her out on a date, not that she would have gone out with me back then."

I congratulated him, wished him luck with Veronica, and thanked him for stopping by with the news. Then I encouraged him to finish off the three remaining oatmeal cookies, which he did in three quick bites. I wished Wyatt a good night and headed cautiously up the stairs, leaving Stone to see the detective out and lock up behind him. I was relieved to see the light on at the top of the landing.

I walked softly so as not to disturb anyone's sleep as I made my way to Stone's suite. Crystal was sleeping in my room, and I had a debt to pay; a promise to Stone that I looked forward to fulfilling.

Stone soon joined me, telling me that Wyatt had departed shortly after I left the kitchen. We chatted for a few minutes about what had been discussed with the detective.

"Did you catch the part about Veronica not having a very good relationship with her father?" Stone asked.

"Yeah, I did. Seems a little odd to me. If she's not particularly concerned about his passing, then why was she so insistent on having a professional and thorough investigation into the murder? Was it just an inheritance she was interested in?"

"I don't know."

"And why did she make a bee-line back to Rockdale? I wonder why she wasn't closer to Horatio than Wyatt thought she had been. Do you think this is a matter we should delve in to a little more deeply?"

"I'm not sure, but somehow I have a feeling that you want to do some delving, and my opinion doesn't really matter." Stone smiled a bit as he spoke. It was not a happy smile, I noticed.

"Oh, dear," I said, as I sighed dramatically. "Your opinion matters very much to me, Stone. But it won't necessarily deter me from tracking Veronica down tomorrow morning."

"I was afraid of that." Stone sighed even more dramatically than I had and turned back the covers of his bed. "Hop in, you little spitfire."

I went to sleep in Stone's arms, with a contented smile on my face, and I slept like a baby for the first time in weeks. It'd been a very exhausting, but satisfying and productive, day.

CHAPTER TWENTY-ONE

I woke up bright and early the next morning, only to find that I was the last one to get out of bed. The Historical Society, minus the deceased and jailed members, were milling around in the kitchen and parlor, drinking coffee and conversing pleasantly with one another. Cornelius had Rosalinda cornered, and Harry and Otto were laughing at something Patty had said. Alma wasn't present, but that didn't surprise me any. Stone was on the back porch discussing something with Detective Johnston again, and Crystal was standing at the stove frying bacon.

I greeted the guests and Crystal before joining Stone and Wyatt on the back porch. The fact that I snatched a cup of coffee off the kitchen counter goes without saying. Stone and Wyatt each had a mug in their hands, as well, as I opened the back door.

"Good morning, gentlemen."

"Good morning," they replied in unison.

"Anything new?" I asked. I assumed the detective had stopped by with some new information regarding the murder investigation.

"Not really," he replied. "Just in the neighborhood and thought I'd stop by. Crystal invited me to stay for breakfast, and I thought I'd take her up on the offer. I wouldn't want to offend her."

I doubted it took much consideration on the detective's part to agree to the invitation and wondered if he hadn't had that exact possibility in mind when he stopped by in the first place. "Glad to have you, Wyatt. You are always welcome here, of course."

"I appreciate it. It's warming up today, isn't it?" he asked. "Looks like it's going to be a mild day. I may ask Veronica out for supper tonight since she's kind of stuck here in town all by herself for a few days."

"That's a good idea. Speaking of Veronica," I said, glad to have an opening to bring her name up in the conversation. "I'd like to speak with her this morning. I want to offer her my condolences, and all that, you know. Do you know where I could find her sometime later after breakfast?"

Wyatt nodded, and after taking a long sip of his steaming coffee said, "Sure. She's staying at the Sands Motel while she's in town. She's in room two fourteen, and I'm sure she'd welcome the company."

"Thanks for stopping by, Ms. Starr."

I grasped Veronica's outstretched hand and shook it. "You're quite welcome and please call me Lexie. Since the murder took place at my boyfriend's establishment, I thought I really ought to come over and offer my sincere condolences. I wish I could tell you there was a solid lead in the case, but I can't."

"I wish you could, too, Lexie. So far I'm not too impressed with the investigation that's taking place on my father's murder case. I'd hoped to be able to make funeral arrangements while I was back here, but the body is tied up pending further investigation."

"Yes, I suppose it is." *The body* sounded a bit impersonal for my taste.

"At least this happened at an opportune time for me," Veronica said. I wondered whether there could ever be an opportune time for a parent to be murdered, but I didn't say anything.

192

"I'm between jobs right now and not too sure what the future holds for me. It's nice to have a reason to take a break from pounding the pavement for a while, looking for employment, but I can't stay here indefinitely."

"I'm just sorry the reason for your break was the loss of your father," I said.

"Yeah, well, whatever. Let's run down to the little café up the street and have some coffee. You do drink coffee, don't you?" Veronica asked.

"I've been known to have a cup now and then."

A few minutes later we were seated at a table in the rear of the café, sipping our coffee. I studied Veronica for a moment and realized she was a stunningly beautiful woman. She had that cheerleader look to her: tall, willowy, blonde, and busty. Her hair reached halfway down her back, and her lipstick was very red around her full pouty lips. I could understand why Detective Johnston was infatuated with her. I doubted she cooked much, however, as she was so thin it appeared she hadn't had a decent meal in weeks. She could use a platter of biscuits and gravy, I thought.

"Have you had breakfast, Veronica?"

"No, I don't do breakfast," she said.

Why did that not surprise me? I hazarded to guess that she really just didn't do food much at all. I decided to bite the bullet and get down to brass tacks. "I hope I'm not being too intrusive, but it seems to me that you weren't all that devastated over the loss of your father. Am I wrong?" I asked, patting her hand resting on the surface of the table. I didn't want to seem as if I were being judgmental. I was, but that's beside the point.

I was surprised to see tears in her eyes as she answered. "No, I guess you could say you aren't wrong. We were never very close, and I feel bad about not being more shaken up over his death than I am. But, you see, my mother died when I was eight. I was torn up and lost without her. But Dad . . . well he just dusted himself off, handed me over to a new nanny, and lined up the next of several wives to come. He never shed a tear, never looked back. He just dove even deeper into his work at D&P Enterprises, and forgot I ever existed. I kind of lost both my parents at the same time."

"I'm so sorry, my dear," I said, trying to comfort her. "I really am."

"Thanks," she said. "I led a very lonely childhood after my mom died. Nannies came and went, waging constant battles with my father and taking it out on me. I know I shouldn't hold a grudge or let bitterness interfere with my life, but I guess I just can't help it. I feel like I grew up as an orphan, and that's tough to get over."

"I'm sure it is. I grew up in a close and warm family atmosphere, so it is hard for me to even imagine how you feel. Why, may I ask, were you so determined to get a private detective before the case got transferred to the county investigative team?"

"That's a long story."

"Go ahead," I encouraged. "I'm in no special hurry."

"My ex-husband is back in town this week from his home in Utah. He's here to attend his class reunion in Leavenworth, which was a couple days ago. He never got along with my father. In fact they hated each other's guts, and I just needed to assure myself that he had nothing to do with Dad's death. He's got kind of a volatile temper."

"Why did they hate each other so much?" I asked.

"When Caleb asked me to marry him, my father was beside himself. He nearly forbade us to marry, and called Caleb a blooming idiot and a worthless bum. Caleb never was much at working or holding a job, and he had a history of drug use, although that was truly in his past. He hadn't touched the stuff since he graduated from college. And he was kind of a career student. It took him seven years to earn a B.A. in business administration, although it was a degree he never utilized. Caleb was a free-spirited guy, and he resented my father's interference in our lives. Caleb was right though. Dad really was a bastard!"

I involuntarily glanced down to check out the size of Veronica's feet. No, her feet were as long as she was tall, so it couldn't have been her small footsteps in the snow outside the inn the morning of the murder.

"Veronica, maybe I can check into this for you. Do you know where Caleb is staying while he's in town? I can go see what information I can get out of him. Perhaps just to give you some peace of mind, if nothing else."

"As far as I can tell, he is staying with his parents in Leavenworth. His parents live on Spruce Street, just a few blocks from the county courthouse at Fourth and Walnut. It's a green ranch home with a red tiled roof."

"Have you seen Caleb since you've been back in town?" I asked.

"No, and I haven't spoken to him either, but I did see a friend of mine who was in his class in high school, and she told me that his current wife did not attend the reunion with him. The reunion took place the night after Dad's murder," Veronica said. "Do you really think you can find out if he has an alibi for that night? It would sure be a relief if you could."

"I'll do my best!"

CHAPTER TWENTY-TWO

It didn't take long to find the lime green ranch house with the red tiled roof once I turned on Spruce. Somehow I'd known it would stand out like a sore thumb, and it did. I parked my Jeep in front of the house and tried to think of some way to approach this matter. I really hadn't given it much thought on my way to Leavenworth. As usual, I was being more impulsive than judicious. Exhibiting deep, sound judgment was not really one of my inherent traits.

I decided to just wing it as I approached the front door. I asked the older woman who answered the door if Caleb was in residence and she nodded.

"Just a sec," she said, leaving with the door still wide open.

When Caleb came to the door with a puzzled look on his face, I paused, dumbstruck. I was staring at the most magnificent human being I had ever seen. This Caleb guy was a handsome sight for sore eyes. He had a body to die for with a face to match. His eyes were almost turquoise, and he had a Caribbean-cruise type tan that he couldn't come by naturally in Salt Lake City in the middle of the winter. Every dark hair on his perfectly shaped head was in place while he waited for me to speak. It took me a moment, however, because I was calculating the difference in our ages and deciding he was young enough to be my son.

"Hello Caleb, I'm Estelle Brady, a reporter with the *Leavenworth Times*. I'm writing an article about the untimely death of your former father-in-law, Horatio Prescott. May I speak with you a minute?"

If Caleb was curious about how I knew Horatio was his former father-in-law or that he was staying at his parent's house in Leavenworth, he didn't show it. I guess one couldn't expect an exquisite body like that to have an ounce of sense.

"Well, no, Ms. Brady, I'm really kind of busy right now," he said. "I've got to head to the airport in less than hour." As Caleb made a move to close the door in my face, I stuck my foot inside and pushed the door open again. As I stepped around him into the hallway I said, "Trust me, this will only take a few minutes of your time, and then I'll be on my way. And please call me Evelyn."

"I thought you said your name was Estelle."

"Uh-oh, did I s-s-say Estelle?" I said, stuttering as I often did when I lied. "I'm really s-s-sorry, I meant Evelyn. My full name is Estelle Evelyn Brady, but most people call me Evelyn," I explained. Good Lord, I had to get this lying stuff down a little better or stop doing it before it got me into deep doo-doo.

"Yeah, okay, Evelyn it is then. What do you need to know?" he asked. "When did Horatio die? What happened to him? Heart attack? Cancer?"

Caleb seemed sincerely surprised at the news of the man's death. If he was lying, he was one hell of an actor.

"He was murdered, actually, several nights ago in Rockdale. He was staying at the Alexandria Inn, there to attend a ceremony in his honor. He was to be inducted as the new president of the Rockdale Historical Society," I explained.

"I'm not surprised," Caleb said, dryly. "He always was a snooty son of a bitch. And a real bastard."

I quickly checked his shoe size, wondering why everybody I met considered Horatio Prescott a real bastard. Did this man have absolutely no friends at all?

"So who shot him?" he asked.

I almost wet myself, thinking for a second that I had just solved the case. I had not mentioned the cause of death to this point, other than that it was a homicide. Horatio could have been poisoned, as he nearly was, or strangled. He could have been stabbed through the heart with an icicle for that matter. How did Caleb know immediately the man was shot?

"Who said he was shot?" I asked.

"I guess I just assumed that," he answered. "If he wasn't shot, then how was he killed?"

"Well, okay, he was shot. Just seemed odd to me you already knew how he was killed."

"Wait a minute, sister!" Caleb had picked up on my inference. "Shooting was just the first and most obvious thing that came to mind. I truly had no idea the man was recently murdered, or even if he was still alive. True, I had no use for the jerk at all, but that part of my life is over. I've moved on and I've never given Prescott or his daughter a second thought. I hate to hear he was murdered, but then again, I am not all that sorry to hear he's gone. He was a self-absorbed, self-serving man, with no regard for anybody but himself."

"Can I quote that?" I said, rather stupidly, suddenly remembering I was there to get information for a newspaper piece. "For my article, you know."

"No, of course not. This conversation is strictly private, Evelyn. I want no part of your article."

That's good, I thought. I wasn't even carrying a pen or pad of paper had he agreed to let me quote him. "Okay, well you do have a confirmable alibi for the night in question, I assume."

"As a matter of fact I do, not that it's any of your business, Ms. Brady. I was at a party all evening, with seven or eight of my former classmates. After the party at Tuna's Bar and Grill in Tonganoxie, we all went to Michael Zarda's house and crashed for the night. I'm sure any or all of them would be happy to confirm my whereabouts," Caleb answered smugly. "I had nothing to do with his death and have a rock solid alibi to back me up!"

Seven or eight witnesses would make for a very solid alibi, I realized. Victoria had been barking up the wrong tree, I was sure. I apologized for the intrusion and headed straight back to the Sands Motel.

"So, you see, Veronica, I don't see how Caleb could have been involved in your father's death," I said. I didn't mention that Caleb had assured me he never gave Veronica or her father a second thought after moving on with his life following their divorce. She'd had enough heartache in her life so far.

"That's a relief," she said, even though she didn't look all that happy with the news. I think she liked the idea of Caleb spending the rest of his days behind bars, out of spite, if nothing else. I wanted to tell her I approved of her taste in men but feared it would be like rubbing salt in a fresh wound.

"Caleb seems like a decent enough man, and he told me to extend his condolences to you on the loss of your father."

Veronica shrugged with indifference and thanked me for tracking down Caleb and questioning him. I told her I was glad to be of assistance and then asked her if she would like to join us at the inn for lunch. "I imagine Stone's housekeeper Crystal will have lunch ready shortly. In fact, I need to get back shortly to help out."

"Thanks, but no. I'm going out to eat supper tonight with a very nice Rockdale detective I have known since high school," she said, with a giddy lilt to her voice.

I was pleased to see she was looking forward to her date with Detective Johnston, but not surprised she had turned down my offer for lunch. I couldn't imagine her eating two meals in the very same day and maintaining that skeletal frame of hers.

CHAPTER TWENTY-THREE

After detailing my visits with Veronica and Caleb to Stone, I decided to join Crystal in the kitchen. I had noticed that all the guests were lounging around in the living room and parlor, and at least half of them were sound asleep. I was careful not to wake them. They were much easier to keep satisfied if they were asleep.

After getting to know them all a little better, I couldn't truly imagine any of them putting a slug into the back of another person's head. I knew it was still just the early stages of the murder investigation, but I was beginning to wonder if all the questions would ever be answered. It seemed as if everyone I spoke with had a motive, but no one was actually guilty of the crime.

Stone and I might have to just sit back and let the future unfold and see if any suspects floated to the surface. We had no investigative training, other than whatever Stone had picked up in his services as a reserve police officer in Myrtle Beach. We were basically just two inquisitive people with an interest in the outcome of the murder investigation because it occurred at the Alexandria Inn.

I shook my head as if to clear my mind and told myself I had to put the murder on the back burner for a spell and get to work in the kitchen. I couldn't dump the entire responsibility of taking care of our guests on Crystal. She'd been putting in enough hours as it was.

I'd wanted to serve lemonade with lunch but had forgotten to take the canisters out of the freezer. They were frozen as solid as an anvil, but I couldn't put them in the microwave because they had tin cylinders on each end. I decided to stick them in the oven, crank up the temperature to near broil, and let the lemonade begin to thaw out while I sliced some tomatoes and shredded some lettuce for the roast beef sandwiches.

Crystal was sitting at the table humming a popular jingle from a television commercial and stirring a big bowl of potato salad. I sat down beside her with a loud sigh. She laughed when I asked, "Didn't these people just finish breakfast a half hour ago?"

"It sure seems like it. I started peeling potatoes for their lunch just two minutes after I finished cleaning up after their breakfast. But, keep in mind, Lexie, they're all leaving just as soon as we can get them fed so let's serve lunch as early as we can. The streets are nearly dry already."

I finished shredding the lettuce and began slicing tomatoes, keeping in mind the lemonade would have to come out of the oven soon, before the heat caused too much pressure to build up inside the containers. I could add warm water to the frozen concentrate once it had thawed enough to slide out of the canisters. And then add ice to cool down the lemonade for drinking.

Crystal was dicing some pickles into the potato salad, and we chatted about inconsequential things as we worked companionably side-by-side. I'd just about finished slicing the final tomato when the paring knife slipped out of my hand and clattered to rest on the floor beneath the table. I scooted my chair back and ducked my head under the tablecloth to reach for the knife.

Before I knew it, I found myself staring at Crystal's feet, clad only in white cotton socks. She had slipped off her loafers as she worked at the table. Why had I never noticed before how badly her right foot was deformed? Was it because I'd never seen her without her shoes on? The entire right half of the upper part of the foot was missing.

"Oh, gosh, Crystal," I said, as I sat upright once again. Before I could think about the intrusiveness of my question, I asked, "Whatever happened to your foot? You poor little thing. Was it an accident of some kind?"

"Yes, it was an accident. My own stupid fault, really. I slid on some wet grass one day as I was mowing the yard, and three of my toes were severed when my foot made contact with the mower blade. They were unable to reattach the severed toes."

"Oh, for gracious sakes! How horrible for you, Crystal. I'm so sorry. No one would ever know by just watching you walk, though. You're more graceful than I am by a long shot."

"Thanks. It's been several years now. I seldom think about it anymore. I had to go through quite a bit of physical therapy following the accident. Once I was able to walk without limping, I wasn't nearly as self-conscious about it. I barely think about it these days."

I nodded absentmindedly. I was thinking about the footprints in the snow I'd photographed the morning after discovering Horatio Prescott had been murdered. Crystal would have driven her car to the inn Sunday morning, parked in the carport, walked across the landscaping stones to the front porch, and used her own key to open the front door of the inn. As the housekeeper, she'd been given a master set of keys and could unlock any door at will.

I thought about her maimed foot again. She would just naturally put more pressure on the left side of the foot than the right, causing a more profound imprint from one side of the shoe than the other. Why hadn't I thought of it before when it had been determined the neighbors were out of town, and the footprints were too small, and the imprint didn't match the department-issued detectives' shoes of the officers who'd responded to Stone's call that morning?

Crystal was in the kitchen when I went downstairs at seven A.M. on Monday. Neither Stone nor I had ever questioned her about what she might have witnessed early Monday morning. Had the Rockdale detectives asked her for a statement? I couldn't recall but didn't think they had. I think she'd been overlooked, as if she were just a fixture in the inn and not a person with potential motives or, at least, observations from Monday morning deserving to be explored by the investigators. I didn't want to think for a single moment Crystal could have any kind of involvement in the murder of Horatio Prescott, but I had to be realistic, and I had to ask her about it whether I wanted to or not.

"Say, Crystal, just out of curiosity, did any of the detectives ask you what time you arrived here on Monday morning?"

"No. Why do you ask?" Crystal sounded dubious.

"Just curious if the detectives ever took a statement from you on what you might have seen or heard Monday morning after reporting for work. What time did you get here, by the way?"

I suddenly noticed Crystal was looking at me in an odd way. There was a definite note of defensiveness in her voice when she asked, "Just what are you getting at, Lexie? You aren't saying you think I might have had something to do with the murder, are you?"

I felt sick to my stomach as I watched fury creep into Crystal's expression. I had never seen her so angry before and noticed now she looked like an entirely different person. I wondered why I hadn't considered her a potential suspect. Whose fingerprints had been found in the room other than the victim's, Stone's and mine? Crystal's had. But since she was the housekeeper, no one had even questioned the presence of her prints in the room. It was Stone and I who set the room up initially, and Sunday was the first night the room had been used by a guest. Why would the housekeeper have even been in the room up to that point?

Thinking back, I didn't think she'd ever had a reason to go upstairs, due to her recent employment at the time. Crystal had only been working at the inn for a day or two when the murder occurred. Up to the time of the murder, Crystal's services had been confined to the first-floor rooms, primarily to the kitchen, library, and parlor. I recalled her mentioning an interest in finding out how the suites had been decorated the day after the murder. So how did her fingerprints come to be in Mr. Prescott's room?

Who would have had the easiest and most frequent opportunities to slip poison into Mr. Prescott's mixed drinks, and then into my coffee the following day? Again the answer was Crystal. Who would have had the easiest opportunity to snatch the manuscript from Prescott's room and place it in Otto's suitcase? The obvious answer again, in my opinion, was Crystal. She could have hidden it in the kitchen cabinet and never even taken it to Otto's room. And why had she become so anxious and upset when I brought up the fact she hadn't been asked for a statement?

The investigators had not done a gunshot residue test on her, either. She'd maintained a low profile in the kitchen and dining room the day the investigators were at the inn testing the guests' hands for signs of gunpowder residue. If I remembered right, she had even had to make a mad dash to the market at about that time. I glanced at her now and saw a vacant expression— the look of someone who'd lost his soul and was acting out of desperation. I had to tread lightly.

"No, of course I don't think you had anything to do with the murder, Crystal. Don't be silly. I was just wondering why you were overlooked as a potential witness, considering you were up and about earlier than about anyone else that morning. Seems to me you could very possibly have seen or heard more than any other person in the inn, aside from the killer."

"Couldn't tell you," Crystal said, with an uncharacteristic snippiness to her voice. "No one asked me if I saw or heard anything, but I didn't, so I didn't feel like I had any information to share with anyone."

Her attitude gave me the urge to respond in kind, which was beyond doubt the stupidest thing I could have done at that point. "Guess you didn't really mind the fact you were being allowed to fly beneath the radar, so to speak. I'm sure you also don't mind that the county homicide team is stopping by the inn this afternoon and planning to perform a gunshot residue test on you while they're here to test Stone and me. They said it's just a formality to test everyone who was present in the inn when the murder occurred. They'd suddenly realized the three of us had been overlooked."

There was absolute evil in Crystal's eyes now. I was sure she was trying to evaluate the truthfulness of my comments. She might have sensed I was just throwing out comments to see how she'd react to them. Crystal could have figured out by now I was putting two and two together and coming up with a "crystal" clear conclusion.

I felt the hairs on the back of my neck bristle. I realized I was in a dangerous position. Crystal turned to me with an expression I'd never seen on her face before. Her lips were curled into a sneer, and she said, "Think you're pretty smart, don't you, Ms. Starr? Were you thinking you just might trick me into an admission?"

"Well, no, of course not, don't be silly—"

"Okay, fine, I'll admit it, Lexie. I killed the greedy son-of-a-bitch—"

"Oh, my God."

"—and as much as I hate it," Crystal continued, "now I'm going to have to kill you, too. I feel badly about it because I really liked you. But, unfortunately, you've given me no choice. For your sake, I truly wish the tansy oil had been effective. It'd have been a lot less messy." Crystal's chest heaved with a heavy sigh. The look on her face indicated that having to kill me too was really inconveniencing her.

"Just out of curiosity, where'd you get the tansy oil, Crystal?" I asked softly.

"From the Dunsten Drug Store in St. Joseph, where I was working when I applied for this job," she said in a matter-of-fact tone.

Now I remembered where I'd seen the name Dunsten Drug Store before. It was on Crystal's resume when she applied for the housekeeper/cook position here at Alexandria Inn.

"But according to the homicide team, there's no record of any tansy oil sales at the store for the last several months."

"No, there wouldn't be any record of a sale. I stole the oil, of course," Crystal said with another sneer. "And who do you think kept the records there? I did. So I altered the inventory list to reflect the decreased amount of tansy oil the store had on hand. I take it no one has ever told you the story about how curiosity killed the cat?"

She reached into the pocket of her apron and whipped out a small derringer handgun. A .32-caliber Derringer, no doubt, I thought with a start. My heart began to hammer inside my chest. Despite the likelihood I was about to be shot, I found it hard to believe Crystal could've already taken another person's life and was now threatening to take mine. Who would've ever imagined this sweet young woman could be a cold-blooded killer? Without thinking, I expressed my surprise at the change in her personality. She suddenly seemed like a person I'd never met before.

"Well, I wasn't the president of the drama club for nothing," she said with sarcasm.

I knew the paring knife I held in my hand was not going to save me. I tossed it down on the kitchen table so Crystal would not view it as a threat. I was going to have to rely on my wits—and maybe some old-fashioned good fortune—to get out of this situation alive.

The house was full of people, and yet it was unlikely another soul was on this end of the dwelling. The house was so large and the walls so thick, even a scream could conceivably go unnoticed. It was worth a try, however.

"Open your mouth to scream, and I'll be forced to shoot," Crystal cautioned, as if she'd read my mind. "I have a silencer on this gun, you know. I can be miles away from here before anyone even realizes you're dead."

Yes, I did know she had a silencer, and I believed she'd shoot if I even looked like I might attempt a scream. She had a desperate look on her face, convincing me she'd do whatever she had to do in a last-ditch effort to avoid being apprehended. She had nothing to lose at this point. I clamped my lips together tightly. If nothing else, it gave me a little confidence to realize Crystal was stalling. She could've shot me and been gone already.

Over her shoulder I saw a whiff of smoke escape from the oven. I heard hissing sounds as drops of the frozen concentrate dripped from one of the canisters and landed on the scalding hot surface below. Crystal was so tense she didn't appear to notice the smoke or hissing sounds coming from the oven. I started to comment on the fact, but stopped myself just in time. Due to the adrenaline pumping through her veins, Crystal was oblivious to what was happening in the oven behind her. I knew I might be able to use her distracted state to my advantage. I had to come up with some kind of stall tactic to buy myself time.

"Why did you kill Mr. Prescott, Crystal?" I asked in as calm a voice as I could manage.

"The greedy bastard destroyed my family."

"How did he destroy your family? What happened? Maybe if you turn yourself in and explain it to the authorities, they'll show leniency toward you."

"No they won't. Don't try to con me, Ms. Starr. I may be young, but I'm not a complete fool."

"I know you're not a fool, Crystal. Don't start being foolish now by killing me, too. You would definitely be caught and tried and found guilty. This is Missouri, you know. They have capital punishment in this state. Kill me too, and you'll be lucky to escape getting the needle," I said. I was trying to reason with her. And if I scared her into handing over her gun, that'd be all right with me. "Is there someone in on this plot with you? Someone who pushed me down the stairs Tuesday night after you'd already left to go home."

"No, there's no one else involved, although I think everyone who knew Prescott is glad to see him gone."

"But then who—"

"I pushed you down the steps. I was hiding behind a cabinet in the storage room attached to Stone's office. I waited a long time for you to come upstairs. Afterwards, I climbed down the emergency fire escape and walked out to my car while everyone was attending to you, lying on the steps. I wasn't really hoping to kill you, just put you out of commission for a while. If you hadn't been so determined to see Peter Randall cleared of the charges against him, you would've had the opportunity to see the sun come up tomorrow. Sometimes being a goody two-shoes isn't such a great idea."

"You'd let an innocent man be charged with a murder you committed and let him be punished for something he didn't do?" I found this more unforgivable than the actual murder.

"Yep. I would've been delighted to see Randall take the fall for Prescott's murder. More than delighted, actually. He was my father's financial advisor at one time, too, for a few years anyway. My father lost a lot of money on his stock tips, not once or twice, but three separate times. As Dad grew poorer, Randall grew richer off the commissions Dad was paying him to make the trades for him. He was nearly as greedy and immoral as Horatio Prescott. You should have backed off and let Randall take the fall. For one thing, you would have lived to see tomorrow."

"If you kill me too, there is no way you'll get away with it. How is it going to help your parents if you end up in prison or worse? The attorney fees will be overwhelming, and having you led away in shackles won't be easy on them either."

I heard the sizzling sound of more drops of lemonade hitting the bottom of the oven. Crystal still seemed oblivious to the sound as she appeared to contemplate what I'd just said and even seemed to consider setting the small handgun down on the table. But then she shook her head and pointed the gun at me with a new resolve.

"They'll get over it and be happy to have achieved retribution. Now back up and get your hands up where I can see them," she said. "Besides, I can't undo what's already been done."

I did as she instructed and asked again, "Why did you kill him, Crystal? What did Prescott do to you? The least you can do is explain it to me before you kill me."

Crystal sighed and said, "My father used to work for him at D&P Enterprises. Dad was a CPA there, head of their accounting department. One day he brought it to Mr. Prescott's attention there was an unexplained deficit of several hundred thousand dollars in the corporate account. Prescott went ballistic."

"Going ballistic" was one of Wendy's favorite sayings. Crystal and Wendy had to be about the same age, I thought. I made a mental note I needed to call Wendy if I lived through this current ordeal. I turned my attention back to Crystal to listen to her explanation.

"Dad was just doing his job, doing what he was paid to do, and yet, a week later he was given his walking papers. Prescott fired him, of course. It became very clear to Dad who was responsible for the missing money."

"Mr. Prescott, I presume?"

Crystal looked annoyed, as if disgusted with me for not paying attention. She said, "Yes, of course it was Prescott. My father had been a loyal employee of D&P Enterprises for over fifteen years when this happened."

"Your father surely had good enough qualifications to get another job somewhere else," I said to the young woman who now had tears streaming from her eyes. It was obviously a very emotional subject for her. I was touched at how deeply she cared for her parents and amazed at just how far she would go for them.

"He was so upset at being fired by Prescott that he suffered a massive stroke that same evening," Crystal said. "He's been in a wheelchair ever since, unable to use his right arm or leg, and he's unable to speak coherently. He draws disability pay, but my mother had to go to work, cleaning other people's houses, to make ends meet. And it's all because of the corruptness of Mr. Prescott, who fired my father because he was afraid Dad would be able to prove he was the one who embezzled the missing money. Dad was convinced both Prescott and Dack were stealing from the company, behind each other's backs, as if competing to see who could out-embezzle the other partner. I vowed to myself one day I would make Mr. Prescott pay for what he did, and Boris Dack, too, if the opportunity arose. I was happy to see Dack brought down without my help. And—"

"Uh-huh," I nodded. "Go on. What'd you do next?" I had to keep Crystal talking.

"When I heard the buffoon was being honored at a dinner here at the inn, and Mr. Van Patten was looking for help, I knew it was the opportune time to exact justice. It was time to make Horatio Prescott pay for the pain and suffering he had forced my family to endure. So I turned in an application, and you interviewed me and selected me for the job. Thanks, by the way, for giving me this opportunity."

"Well, you did have the best qualifications of all the applicants," I said inanely.

"Thanks," Crystal said with a smile. "I took over all of the responsibilities of running the household when my mother had to go to work to support us. Not only did I learn how to take care of the family finances, I also learned how to cook, sew, clean, and even—"

Crystal stopped talking abruptly, realizing she'd drifted away from the main subject. She waved the gun recklessly and continued to speak. "Anyway, I was hoping to eliminate Mr. Prescott by poisoning him. But, as you know, that plan failed, as did my attempt to eliminate you the same way when you started asking too many questions. I realized too late, unfortunately, I should've given Horatio the entire dose of the tansy oil. If I had, all that's followed wouldn't have even been necessary."

Crystal was now sobbing and the gun was oscillating back and forth in her quivering hand. I really did feel sorry for what had happened to make this young woman so bitter, even though she was threatening my life for the third time since Monday. This obsession of hers was beginning to irritate me, but I had to appear as if I felt nothing other than an overwhelming compassion for her.

"I'm so sorry, Crystal, for you and your entire family. Now

that I've heard your story, I'm sure the authorities would show leniency. They might actually acquit you of the murder charge, if you were to turn yourself in before anyone else gets hurt. I promise I'd help you in any way I can." I was sincere in my pledge. I was not merely trying to save my own life, although it did add a compelling incentive.

Puffs of smoke were now coming from around the door of the oven on a regular basis, and drops of lemonade concentrate continued to drip and fizzle on the bottom of the oven. As ridiculous as it seemed, I felt bad about making a mess in the new oven Stone had recently purchased for the inn. I wondered if Easy Off Oven Cleaner could remove the burnt residue from the bottom of the oven. It occurred to me then that I must have taken complete leave of my senses to be worried about the oven when I was in imminent danger of losing my life.

"I'm afraid I can't trust you. I can't trust anyone. I'm sorry, but I have no choice but to eliminate you as a threat, Lexie. If it's any consolation, I really do feel bad about having to kill you." With trembling hands, Crystal lifted the gun and aimed it at my face. She grimaced and squinted her eyes, as if she couldn't stand to watch the bullet pierce my skull. As she began to squeeze the trigger, she closed her eyes tightly shut.

I tensed my muscles and shut my eyes tightly, too, no more thrilled about the situation than Crystal claimed to be.

Ka-boom!

The loud explosion rocked the kitchen of the Alexandria Inn and could be heard from one end of the old historic home to the other. The loud percussion of the shot knocked me off the chair and on to the tiled floor.

"Aaggghhhh!" A scream followed in the wake of the explosion. My first thought was I felt pretty good for someone who'd just been shot. My second thought was it had been a loud explosion for a gun with a silencer attached to it. And my third thought was it had actually been Crystal who'd screamed, not me. I opened my eyes slowly, relieved to discover I'd not been shot at all. The explosion had come from the oven, not the gun Crystal had been brandishing. The gun now lay on the floor, where it'd been flung as Crystal was hit by flying debris.

A thick cloud of smoke enveloped the young woman as hot lemonade dripped from her skin and shards of glass from the oven door stuck out at all angles from her back and arms. Crystal groaned, writhing in agony from the burns and lacerations she'd sustained from the exploding lemonade canister. One of the lemonade canisters had finally built up too much pressure in the severe heat of the oven, I realized. It was the miracle I had been praying for.

I was sprawled out on the floor in complete astonishment for a few moments before I pulled myself to my feet to do a quick assessment of my condition. I had a few drops of hot sticky lemonade juice on my forearm, and felt the sharp pain of a rather large shard of glass piercing my left shoulder. And I was still bruised and sore from my ungraceful fall down the stairs.

But all in all, it wasn't nearly bad enough to prevent me from lunging for the derringer that had clattered loudly as it fell onto the floor beneath the table, immediately following the explosion. As I snatched the gun from the floor, the kitchen door sprang open and Stone rushed into the room. It was evident he was startled to see I was clutching a gun in my hands and also by the fact there was blood flowing out of both Crystal and me. Despite her injuries, Crystal made a dash for the door leading to the veranda, nearly knocking over Stone in her haste.

"It was Crystal. She killed Mr. Prescott, Stone. Stop her!" I yelled. I knew I looked and sounded like a raving lunatic, with blood and lemonade dripping from me as I shouted at Stone.

Stone looked at me searchingly. I nodded and gestured toward the door with Crystal's gun. He sighed, took a deep breath, and bolted for the door with me right behind him. In an awkward series of motions, he leaped over several bushes, hurdled a birdbath, and dodged four or five low-hanging tree limbs. Somehow, Stone managed to tackle the fleeing woman before she cleared the yard. The fact Crystal was seriously injured from the lemonade canister explosion no doubt gave Stone a slight advantage.

An enormous sense of relief flooded through me. I was trembling all over in reaction to what had just occurred. I looked up as a crowd of Historical Society members began to gather around me. I realized, suddenly, how thankful I was that no one in our little group of eccentric, but likeable, guests was a hard-hearted killer. I was almost disappointed they'd all be leaving to go home soon. Almost—but not quite.

EPILOGUE

It was with a great deal of sadness that I watched Detective Johnston snap the cuffs onto Crystal's wrists and read her the Miranda Rights. I wished I could have taken notice of her fragile emotional state and found professional help for her before her bitterness and anger had escalated to the point of murder. But I couldn't allow myself to feel personally responsible for her plight. She'd hidden her feelings so well that I'm not sure anyone could've guessed the depth of her mental anguish. There are so many avenues she could've taken in lieu of killing Horatio Prescott, if only she'd reached out for help and not taken justice into her own hands. Unfortunately, like so many others, Crystal had decided to mete out her own justice, in her own violent way. Now justice would be meted out once again—with her on the receiving end. This was not the way I had wanted this murder investigation to end.

I said a quick prayer on her behalf. I prayed the justice system would take pity on her and find she was guilty by reason of insanity, placing her in a mental institution instead of prison. Maybe then she could get the support and counseling she needed and go on to lead a rewarding and productive life.

I gasped in an involuntary reaction as the medical technicians attended to my wound. Soon my attention was averted by Stone's approach. He came up beside me and placed his hand on mine to comfort me.

"Are you doing okay, honey?" he asked. His face turned a

pastel shade of green as he watched an EMT delicately remove the shard of glass imbedded in my shoulder. Blood gushed out after the glass was extracted. The emergency technician handed Stone a large cotton pad and asked him to apply pressure to the wound to staunch the blood flow.

"Yes, I'll be fine, at least after my nerves calm down. How about you? Are you okay?" I asked. I'd noticed he was walking with a slight limp.

He laughed, good-naturedly, and said, "It's just a strained muscle. I'm a little out of shape to be sprinting across the yard, leaping over shrubs and flowerbeds in a single bound, and tackling a young woman who's thirty years younger than I. But, all in all, I'm not too bad."

"I was impressed with your speed and agility, Superman," I said in jest. Stone made a comical face, and we both chuckled. He knew I often had to laugh to keep from crying, and I'd been sincerely fond of Crystal. "I'm just thankful you didn't have to catch a bullet with your teeth," I quipped.

"Me, too, honey. At my age, false teeth are probably just around the corner as it is. I still can't believe it was Crystal. Who'd have ever thought she could commit a murder like that. Shoot a man at point-blank range? And then threaten to shoot you. I can't even imagine her poisoning you or pushing you down a flight of stairs. She seemed so sweet and innocent to me."

"Me, too. I'm as shocked as you are, Stone. But other than her obsession to exact revenge for the harm done to her family, I think she's probably a sincerely sweet, innocent, and thoughtful young lady. Her threat to shoot me was just a panicky reaction borne out of desperation, I'm sure. I'm not convinced she could have actually pulled the trigger and shot me had the lemonade can not exploded when it did. Do you think the justice system will go easy on her?"

He squeezed my hand and kissed my forehead before responding. "I hope so. Detective Johnston has promised me he'd look after her and try to ensure she's treated with compassion and understanding, if that's of any consequence. I think he'll do his best to uphold his promise."

"I do, too. He seems like a man of honor and principles," I said.

"He also just told me Veronica is moving back to the area because after her divorce, she has nothing to keep her in Salt Lake City. Wyatt was pretty tickled about the news."

"Maybe something good will come out of this, after all. It'd be nice to see Wyatt find a mate in Veronica. I hope she likes to cook."

"Yeah, Wyatt deserves a good wife, whether it is Veronica or some other gal. Which reminds me. Did I tell you Cornelius asked me about reserving the entire Alexandria Inn for the last weekend in May?"

"No, why would he want to do that?"

"He said he just asked Rosalinda Swift to marry him, and she's accepted his proposal," Stone said.

"My goodness! Well, how wonderful for both of them!"

"They want to have the rehearsal dinner, the wedding, the reception, the whole works right here at the inn, where they discovered their love for each other. They even plan to spend their wedding night here, along with a number of the guests who'll be coming from out-of-state for the wedding. And Cornelius tells me Rosalinda has agreed to seek help for her alcohol addiction. She'll be attending her first AA meeting tomorrow night, in fact."

"That's terrific news, Stone. I really am happy for them. I hope she can overcome the alcoholism. Then maybe she can keep Horny Corny, the old sex pistol, in check."

"And they haven't scheduled the date yet, but the Poffenbargers are going to reserve the inn one weekend in June. They want to renew their wedding vows and got the idea to do it here at the inn from Cornelius and Rosalinda. Otto told me he's going to be the one to wear the pants in the family this time around. Patty is going to join the Jenny Craig program in town to help her with the weight loss."

"Oh, I'm so happy for them all. It's about time Otto took a stand, isn't it? You know, Stone, I don't think this grand-opening fiasco will hurt the future success of the Alexandria at all. It may even turn out to be a draw—people coming here out of curiosity or morbid fascination. Just think of how popular it'd be if we could get it billed as a haunted house?" Stone laughed with me at the idea. But already the wheels in my mind were turning. I could surely come up with a haunted house concept for the inn to attract customers in October, at least.

"You may be right, honey," he said. "Human nature makes people react in odd ways," he said. "This sure has been an unbelievable and unforgettable grand opening for the Alexandria Inn, don't you think?"

"It sure has. If the first week was this exciting, what do you think the second week will be like?" I asked.

"With any luck at all, it will be boring and uneventful."

"Gee, do you really think so?"

"No, not really," Stone replied, with a chuckle and a shake of his head. "Something tells me as long as you're around, my life will never be boring and uneventful."

"I'll see to it that it isn't. I promise!"

ABOUT THE AUTHOR

Jeanne Glidewell lives with her husband, Robert, in the small town of Bonner Springs, Kansas. She enjoys writing, reading, fishing, and wildlife photography, but her real love is traveling. She has enjoyed many cruises and traveled to countries around the world on five different continents. She volunteers as a Life Mentor with the Gift of Life Program in Kansas City. As a kidney and pancreas transplant patient herself, she mentors people on the organ waiting list prior to their transplants. Jeanne has written numerous magazine articles and a mainstream fiction novel, titled *Soul Survivor,* which is to be released in February 2011. She is a member of Sisters-in-Crime and Mystery Writers of America. Jeanne's first Lexie Starr mystery, *Leave No Stone Unturned,* was published in 2008. She is currently working on another Lexie Starr mystery novel. To contact her visit her Web site at http://www.jeanneglidewell.com.